You're in for a Scare!

CREEPOVER ™

What a Doll!

written by P. J. Night

SIMON SPOTLIGHT

New York London Toronto Sydney New Delhi

This book is a work of fiction. Any references to historical events, real people, or real places are used fictitiously. Other names, characters, places, and events are products of the author's imagination, and any resemblance to actual events or places or persons, living or dead, is entirely coincidental.

SIMON SPOTLIGHT
An imprint of Simon & Schuster Children's Publishing Division
1230 Avenue of the Americas, New York, New York 10020
Copyright © 2013 by Simon & Schuster, Inc.
All rights reserved, including the right of reproduction in whole or in part in any form.
SIMON SPOTLIGHT and colophon are registered trademarks of Simon & Schuster, Inc.
YOU'RE INVITED TO A CREEPOVER is a trademark of Simon & Schuster, Inc.
Text by Kama Einhorn
For information about special discounts for bulk purchases, please contact Simon & Schuster Special Sales at 1-866-506-1949 or business@simonandschuster.com.
Manufactured in the United States of America 0113 OFF
First Edition 10 9 8 7 6 5 4 3 2 1
ISBN 978-1-4424-5985-4
ISBN 978-1-4424-5986-1 (eBook)
Library of Congress Catalog Card Number 2012939908

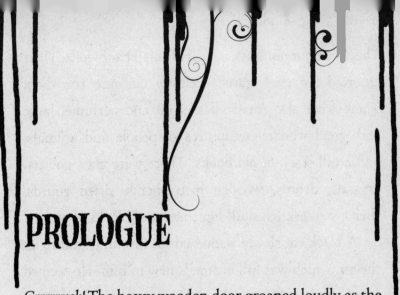

PROLOGUE

Crrrrrreak! The heavy wooden door groaned loudly as the old woman opened it.

It was time to get started.

She lit a few candles and carefully went to work. Her long, straggly white hair swayed across her back as she slowly wiped the dust from each shelf.

The room was dark and small with no windows. The woman removed her wares from their boxes and dusted each item carefully before putting it on a shelf.

First, a shelf of candles in every color, shape, and size. The glass countertop was where the jewelry went— bracelets, necklaces, and earrings that jingle-jangled when you moved around. There were containers of beads for making your own jewelry, beads in every hue.

Then, last but not least, a shelf of small cloth dolls. Their embroidered eyes stared lifelessly out into the shop. There were also small vials of oil and perfume, large and small wooden sculptures of people and animals, and a tall stack of old books. There were glass goblets, crystals, drums, wooden instruments, dried gourds, shells, snakeskins, skull figurines, and blocks of wax.

A black cat slowly wandered in, carefully sniffing at the air, which was full of smells new to him. He seemed startled when he saw the old woman, and arched his back and hissed loudly. The woman, seeming aggravated, stomped one foot, shooing him out of the room.

Once the cat had scampered out, the woman sighed loudly, then put her lamp on the counter and plugged it in. It had a red velvet shade with fringe around the edges.

She turned the lamp on and the room glowed red. She was ready now. Ready for the first poor soul who wandered in.

CHAPTER 1

One Friday night Lizzy Draper and Emmy Spencer were watching TV and eating popcorn at Lizzy's house. This was because Lizzy didn't seem to want to do anything else.

"Pass the popcorn, Lizzy?" Emmy asked her best friend.

Lizzy passed the bowl over with a slightly annoyed look. "It's Liz, remember?" she asked Emmy. "Now that I'm not five anymore?"

"Oh, right. Sorry, Liz," Emmy mumbled. Emmy had a bad feeling in her stomach, the same feeling she'd been having for a few months now. Things were different between the lifelong best friends. There was no denying it. It was simple: Now that they were in seventh grade, Lizzy had become popular, and Emmy had not. Lizzy was talking to boys, and Emmy was not. Lizzy was wearing lip gloss, and Emmy was not. Lizzy—

"Hey, you know something?" Lizzy interrupted Emmy's thoughts. "You could maybe start going by a more mature name yourself."

"What do you mean? Change my name?" Emmy said.

"No, silly," Lizzy said. "Just go by something like Em. Or Emma."

"Em might be okay," Emmy responded. "But my full name's not Emma. It's Emily."

"Right, but Emma is much cooler," Lizzy said, looking totally serious.

"I kind of like Em," said Emmy. "But it would take some getting used to. Hey, I know. Instead of Liz, I could call you Lizard." Emmy laughed at her own joke.

"Like when I was three?" Lizzy asked sarcastically.

Emmy thought it might be a good idea to change the subject. "So what are we going to be for the costume party this year?"

Lizzy paused and examined the pattern on the rug. "Oh," she said. "I was going to tell you. I'm going to do a group costume with Cadence and Sophie."

Ouch. Emmy tried to keep the hurt out of her voice. "But we had so much fun last year," she said.

The costume party was part of their school's spirit week, which was only a few weeks away. When Lizzy and Emmy were in sixth grade, they heard rumors about how competitive some of the kids got with their costumes, and they were a little scared to participate. But then Emmy had the most brilliant idea: Lizzy could dress up as a bug and Emmy could go as a can of bug spray. Lizzy had loved it and so had everyone else. They even won an honorable mention for such a creative costume—an honor very few sixth graders ever received.

Emmy had been thinking of ideas for this year's costume for months now, but apparently it was all for nothing. At this moment, Emmy was feeling a lot like she was an actual bug and Lizzy was the spray.

"I know," Lizzy said. "Sorry."

Lizzy's mom, Marilyn, poked her head into the family room. "You girls should turn off the TV soon," she said.

"There's nothing else to do, Mom," Lizzy said with a hint of a whine. Emmy couldn't help but notice that Lizzy had stopped calling her mother "Mommy," which Emmy still called her mother. What was with all these name changes?

"I can't believe my ears," her mom said. "You two have always found fun things to do together at your sleepovers." It was true. They'd make crazy concoctions in the kitchen, pretend to open up a beauty parlor, write short plays and perform them for their parents, carve bars of soap into funny shapes, and do plenty of other creative stuff.

Lizzy sighed loudly and said nothing more, finally turning off the television when it was time for dinner. The two girls sat silently at the table they had sat at together so many times before, since they were babies in high chairs. Their moms had met when they were pregnant with Lizzy and Emmy, and because they were next-door neighbors on a street deep in the heart of Brooklyn, New York, they spent countless hours with their baby girls in their kitchens, out running errands, at the playground, and even on family vacations together. Lizzy and Emmy had always been inseparable, just like their moms. Until lately.

Twirling spaghetti on her fork, Emmy was lost in thought. How could she feel so lonely with her best friend beside her? Maybe it was because they weren't really best friends anymore. That thought made her so sad she dropped her fork on her plate. It was all she could do to keep herself from putting her head down on the table.

"What's the matter, Emmy?" Marilyn asked.

"Nothing," Emmy said. There was a time when she could tell Marilyn anything, and this wasn't that time. Marilyn and Joanne, Emmy's mom, had always depended on each other to take care of the other's daughter in a pinch. If Joanne couldn't get away from work and Emmy was sick at school, Marilyn would pick her up at the school nurse. If Marilyn had to go to a meeting out of town, Joanne would watch Lizzy until she got back. It was like each girl had two moms. Of course, it was even better than that because it was also like each girl had a sister—Lizzy was an only child, and Emmy had a little brother.

Living next door to each other had always been so much fun. The best part of all was that they could see right into each other's bedrooms. They had all sorts of fun with this, shining laser lights or flashlights on each other's walls in the dark and throwing things back and forth through their open windows. They did have one rule they agreed upon long ago, though: no spying.

As the girls cleared the dishes, Emmy noticed Lizzy looking at her closely. She seemed to be focused on

Emmy's long dark hair, which she wore in two braids. On the way up the stairs to Lizzy's room, Lizzy swished one of Emmy's braids like a horse's tail.

"I have a great idea," Lizzy said as they entered her room. "Let's give you a makeover."

Emmy was pleased that Lizzy wanted to do something, *anything*, with her. And they had played with makeup before. They used to love playing dress-up and putting on fashion shows for their parents. It would be fun. *This sleepover isn't going to be totally awful after all*, Emmy thought.

"Awesome," Emmy said, smiling. "Where's your mom's makeup case?" It was what they'd always used when they played dress-up.

"No makeup," Lizzy announced, swishing Emmy's other braid. "Hair."

"Oh. Okay," Emmy said, and removed the rubber band from each braid. She ran her fingers through her braids to undo them, splaying out her long pretty hair over her shoulders. Her hair was so long it almost reached her butt.

Lizzy looked at Emmy's hair thoughtfully. "I have a vision," she said, grinning, and left the room. "I'll be right back."

Emmy sat cross-legged on the floor, facing the mirror. She couldn't wait to see what Lizzy was going to do. Would she weave a sophisticated inside-out French braid, like she did so well? Use a curling iron? She was so relieved that Lizzy seemed more like her old self that she didn't notice what Lizzy was holding in her hand when she came back into the room.

Scissors.

Lizzy help them up like a magician's wand. "You're going to look great, Em," she promised.

Emmy's heart stopped. "Um, L-Liz . . . ," she stammered. "I don't want an actual haircut. I thought you were just going to braid it or something."

"But haven't you noticed how badly you need one?" Lizzy asked. "We're in seventh grade now, but your hair is stuck in fourth."

Emmy instinctively put her hands to her hair to protect it. What would her mother say if she came home with her hair cut off? She loved her daughter's long hair. So did Emmy, actually. She loved feeling it cover her back, she loved brushing it, she loved braiding it herself. She'd never wanted shorter hair. For her entire life Emmy had never allowed it to be cut more than an inch to get rid of split ends. It had always been long. And so had Lizzy's light blond hair until this year, when she'd gone for a short cut that she described as "sassier than long hair."

Emmy was still stammering. "P-Plenty of grown-ups have long hair," she pointed out.

Lizzy frowned. "Oh, never mind," she said. "You're hopeless."

"I'm sorry," Emmy said, making sure her voice didn't crack. She was on the verge of tears. Things had been so much better in the last few minutes, and now Lizzy was disappointed. She was giving up on Emmy.

"Whatever," Lizzy said like she really didn't care. "I was just trying to help you. Forget it. Let's just go watch TV again."

Emmy's heart sank deeper into her stomach. Her mind raced. Was there some way to salvage this sleepover? Yes, there was.

"How about if you just trim it?" Emmy asked. "I don't mind having it cut a little bit. It might be . . . cool," she added.

Lizzy smiled. "Excellent," she said. "It *will* be cool. I promise. First let me wash it in the sink, like at a real hair salon."

They went into the bathroom, where Lizzy gently sudsed up Emmy's hair and carefully rinsed it. Then she even added conditioner. Emmy loved the feeling of Lizzy's hands massaging her scalp. Lizzy was right. It was just like being at the salon. All the while, Lizzy was humming happily. It was just like old times. She helped Emmy stand up, wrapped one towel around her head and one around her shoulders, and led her back into her bedroom, where she combed out her hair and turned Emmy away from the mirror. Emmy felt like she was at a fancy spa.

"Here, sit on this towel," Lizzy said, "so we don't get hair all over the floor." Emmy moved onto the towel.

Just as Lizzy started cutting, her cell phone rang. She put down the scissors and grabbed the phone.

"Hey, Cadence!" she said happily. "What's up? No, I'm not doing anything."

Yes you are, Emmy thought sadly.

But Lizzy continued the conversation for a few more minutes before hanging up. Then she continued cutting. Emmy was faced away from the mirror, but it felt to her like Lizzy was cutting off quite a lot.

"I think you're cutting too much," she said to Lizzy. "Let me just see in the mirror."

Lizzy put the scissors down and put her hands on her hips. "Do you trust me or not?" she said.

"I trust you," Emmy lied.

Lizzy continued snipping away, stopping twice to check text messages, which she smiled at but did not say anything about.

More snipping. A lot more snipping, actually.

"Okay, you can look now," Lizzy said proudly. And for the next few moments, everything went in slow motion for Emmy.

She turned around slowly and looked in the mirror. It was a bit dark in Lizzy's room, but what Emmy saw was plenty. And her reflection made her scream.

CHAPTER 2

"What, you don't like it?" Lizzy asked blankly, standing next to her in the mirror and looking on. "I think it looks cool."

Emmy held her hands to her mouth in horror. She was silent but still screaming inside. She barely recognized herself in her reflection.

Her hair was short. *Short* short. It barely touched her shoulders. And there were *bangs*, which she'd never wanted, and had never had.

She could barely speak. "I thought you were just going to trim it," she croaked.

"Well, you did need a little more than a trim, Em," Lizzy said calmly.

Emmy could only repeat herself. "I thought you were

just going to trim it. I thought you were just going to trim it," she kept saying, never taking her eyes off her reflection.

"Here, get up," was all Lizzy said. "Let me clean up all these clumps of old hair." She brought the towel, now piled with Emmy's hair, into the bathroom, where she shook it into the garbage as if it was something as ordinary and unimportant as kitchen scraps.

Between then and the time they went to bed, time passed in a strange way. Emmy felt totally vulnerable without all her hair. And every time she passed the mirror, she had a horrible feeling inside, like her stomach was melting.

They went downstairs for a snack and to say good night to Lizzy's parents.

"Oh my!" was Marilyn's response. She couldn't keep the shock off her face.

"It looks great, right?" Lizzy said casually, calmly slicing a banana into the blender for a smoothie. "I did it," she added proudly.

"Well, yes, it's very nice," Marilyn said. "What do *you* think, Emmy?"

Emmy said nothing as she felt her eyes well up with

tears. *I will not cry, I will not cry, I will not cry,* she told herself. Marilyn must have noticed, though, because she put her hand on Emmy's shoulder and squeezed it. Then she tried to catch Lizzy's eye, but Lizzy was busy with the smoothie.

"You want a purple cow, right?" Lizzy asked Emmy. It was their name for their favorite smoothie, which was made with bananas, frozen blueberries, and soy milk. It was named after the poem they had chanted in first grade:

> *I never saw a purple cow*
> *I never hope to see one.*
> *But I can tell you anyhow*
> *I'd rather see than be one.*

They'd loved that poem, and when they first made up the smoothie and admired its purple color, they knew right away what it had to be called. But Lizzy saying "purple cow" now just made Emmy sad. First grade had been so much fun. They had been in the same class and won a jump rope championship. It was all so simple. Both of them had matching long hair then. And they were, as they used to say, "bestest friends."

Emmy tried to smile. "Sure," she said as Lizzy got

out two glasses and bendy straws. Lizzy turned on the blender and, for a minute, the noise distracted Emmy from her sad thoughts. Lizzy poured some purple cow into each cup and handed Emmy one. They stood at the kitchen counter with Marilyn looking carefully at them both, trying to figure out what to say.

Emmy didn't sleep much that night. She was painfully aware that her hair wasn't spread out across her pillow as usual. Her head felt so funny without the weight of her hair on it. She replayed the haircut scene over and over again in her head. How could Lizzy have cut off so much hair? What had she been thinking? Was she secretly mad at Emmy and trying to do something mean? Emmy tried to think of reasons why Lizzy would be mad at her, but couldn't think of any.

She finally fell asleep and had a terrible dream about giant scissors chasing her around her empty school.

When she woke up in the morning, still half asleep, she remembered the dream. It was interesting that the school had been empty in the dream, because that's sort of how school felt to Emmy these days. Empty of fun, empty of laughter, empty of friends. The other girls she used to be friends with seemed to be less interested in hanging out with her than with Lizzy. And Lizzy was adjusting to her new popularity very naturally.

Lizzy was already downstairs. Emmy was alone, with an odd feeling that she'd missed half the day. The room was filled with late-morning light. For a few wonderful seconds Emmy did not remember the haircut. It was only when she sat up and didn't feel her long hair on her shoulders that she remembered. The thought was like a big *thud*.

She sat up and crawled over to the mirror, where it all came rushing back. It had really happened. It was as real as real could be. She looked like a different person! She started down the stairs slowly, and as she reached the bottom she saw Lizzy heading out the front door.

"Hey," she said, a little confused. Where was Lizzy going? Weren't they about to have breakfast together?

Lizzy turned around. "Oh, hey," she said. "I thought I'd let you sleep, sleepyhead. My mom called your mom and told her you'd come home when you got up."

"Where are you going?" Emmy asked.

"I didn't tell you?" Lizzy asked, distracted.

Emmy saw there was a car outside waiting, but she

couldn't tell who was in it. "Tell me what?"

"Cadence and her parents are taking me and Sophie to Manhattan today!" Lizzy squealed. "We're going to go shopping and then see a Broadway show tonight! But first we're going to pick some fresh strawberries at a real farm nearby. They're going to be so delicious."

"Oh," Emmy said. She didn't know what else to say. She stood there in her pajamas and short hair, feeling totally idiotic. "Well, have fun."

"Okay, thanks! Bye!" As Lizzy walked out to the car, Emmy noticed Cadence in the front seat and Sophie in the back. Lizzy shut the car door and did not wave to Emmy.

Emmy went back upstairs to get dressed as quickly as she could. She tried to avoid the mirror this time. What would her mother say? Well, she'd find out soon enough.

On her way out, Emmy passed Lizzy's parents in the kitchen.

"Good morning, Emmy," Marilyn said when she saw her. "It's too bad Liz had to leave so early, but why don't you sit down and have some breakfast?"

"Thanks," Emmy mumbled. "But I've gotta get home. Busy day today." She suddenly couldn't wait to get out of there.

Marilyn gave Emmy a look. "Are you okay, honey?" she asked, her face wrinkled up with concern and sympathy.

"Yeah, thanks," Emmy said quickly. Marilyn had to know that Emmy was seriously hurt by Lizzy's behavior, but Emmy didn't want to start crying in front of Lizzy's parents. That would be embarrassing. And her new "haircut" was embarrassing enough.

Emmy walked to her house next door. As soon as she let herself in and sat on the couch in the living room, her mom came out of the kitchen and gasped. Emmy put her head in her hands.

"What on earth have you done?" her mother said slowly and quietly, the way she sounded when she was absolutely furious. "What have you done to your beautiful hair? If you wanted a change, why didn't you say anything about it?"

"She said she was just going to trim it!" Emmy cried, and this time she didn't hold back her tears.

Her mom softened and joined Emmy on the couch, taking her into a big warm hug. As Emmy cried and cried, her mom just kept saying "Oh, honey."

When Emmy finally stopped crying, she rested

her head on her mom's shoulder, exhausted.

"Honey, I know those tears can't be just about your hair," her mom said. "Did something else happen at Lizzy's?"

Again the tears came. Emmy managed to choke out the whole story: how Lizzy wanted to be called Liz and wanted to call her Em or Emma, how she wanted to "update" Emmy's look, how she took off in the morning with her cool new friends with barely a good-bye and definitely didn't want her to join them. Her mom sighed.

"Honey, I'm afraid this is all normal," she said to Emmy. "You two are at an age where you're growing and changing at different paces and in different ways."

"You mean Lizzy's more *mature* than me," Emmy said, and cried even harder.

"No, she's just exploring different interests," her mom said gently.

"Right," said Emmy. "Except that she's more mature than me and I'm just a big loser."

Just then Emmy's seven-year-old brother, Sam, came downstairs in his soccer uniform, stopping short when he saw Emmy's hair. No matter that Emmy was clearly upset and being comforted by their mom, Sam burst into hysterical laughter and pointed to Emmy's hair.

"Really, Sam." Emmy's mom sighed. "Please. Emmy is obviously upset about this."

"What happened?" Sam asked.

"Lizzy cut it," Emmy told him. "She said she was just going to trim it."

"Oh," Sam said. He really was trying to be good. He turned and went quietly up the stairs, leaving Emmy and her mom alone again.

Emmy turned to her mom. "You and Marilyn have been best friends forever," Emmy said. "And I thought Lizzy and I would be best friends forever too. I don't know what's going on. It's like I'm just not cool enough for her anymore."

"I'm sorry, honey," her mom said. Her mom really was a good listener. But Emmy felt not one little bit better and couldn't wait until it was time to go to sleep. How many more hours before bedtime? Then again, at that point she'd be even closer to showing up at school on Monday with her short, horrible hair.

"I bet I'll get teased on Monday," Emmy murmured to her mom.

Her mom shook her head. Then she said, "And

the good news is that your hair will grow back. In the meantime, how about if we go to my hair salon and have Josephine fix it up a little bit? I bet she'll be able to turn it into a really stylish cut and you'll like it a lot more."

The possibility of actually improving the hair situation hadn't really occurred to Emmy. "Yeah," she said. "That sounds like a good idea."

"Great," her mom said. "I'll call and see if she has any time for an appointment today." She got up and went to the phone in the kitchen. Emmy could hear her mom speaking in a low voice, as if she didn't want Emmy to overhear. *What could she be saying?* Emmy wondered. *The girl that my daughter thought was her best friend just butchered her hair, and can you please fix it by the time she has to show up at school on Monday so she isn't the laughing stock of the seventh grade?*

"Wonderful," Emmy heard her mom say. "We'll see you soon, then." She came back into the living room and smiled at Emmy. "We can go right now," she said. "Josephine will squeeze you in."

So Emmy and her mom walked the four blocks to the salon, where Josephine greeted them tactfully, pretending not to be shocked by what she saw before her. She ran her fingers through what was left of Emmy's hair.

"Not quite what you were expecting, huh?" she asked Emmy sympathetically.

Emmy nodded sadly.

"Well, I definitely think I can work with this," Josephine said to Emmy and her mom. "Come on in and let's get started."

Josephine had Emmy put a robe on over her shirt and then shampooed her hair, just like Lizzy had done yesterday. Emmy had a strange feeling of déjà vu and hoped this haircut would end a little differently than the last one.

It didn't take Josephine long to reshape Emmy's hair into a much better cut. It was still short, but the jagged edges were gone and it looked a lot less awkward. It would take some getting used to having such short hair, but Emmy supposed she could live with it until it grew out.

Sunday was lame.

It rained, and Emmy stayed in her pajamas all day and refused an invitation from her parents to go to a movie. She even took her lunch up to her room and ate it under the covers. *Wouldn't it be great,* she thought, *to be a bear and hibernate for a few months, till my hair has grown out a little? And maybe that'd make Lizzy miss being friends with me?*

She kept thinking Lizzy would call or come by, like she used to on rainy days. So when the doorbell rang, Emmy's heart leapt like an eager dog. She let her mom answer the door.

"Marilyn, hi!" she heard her mom say. So it wasn't Lizzy. It was Lizzy's mom. She heard them speaking softly as though they didn't want Emmy to overhear. Then her mom called upstairs.

"Emmy, honey, come down and say hello to Marilyn."

Emmy didn't know why she suddenly felt so furious with Marilyn. She'd always loved Marilyn just like a second mom. And Marilyn had always treated her like a daughter. But now she felt betrayed. Look what had happened under Marilyn's roof! Under Marilyn's supervision! Still, she knew she had to go downstairs, so she did.

"Hi, Marilyn," she said, avoiding her eyes.

"Hi, Emmy," Marilyn said kindly. "How are you doing? I see you had your hair touched up a little bit. It looks great."

"I'm okay," Emmy said, trying to sound normal.

"Thanks. Yeah, my hair came out okay, I guess."

"I brought you over some of the strawberries that Lizzy picked yesterday," Marilyn said. "She feels really bad that you don't seem to like the haircut."

Then why didn't she come over herself and say so? Lizzy screamed in her head. *Or even send me a text?* But she said nothing.

"Well, Lizzy did say she was just going to trim it, and look how short she cut it," Emmy's mom said, running her fingers through what was left of her daughter's hair. For a moment no one said anything, and the sentence hung in the air. You could cut the tension in the room with a knife. *Great,* Emmy thought. *Now not only are Lizzy and I not best friends anymore, it's causing problems between our moms.*

"I know, Joanne." Marilyn sighed. "I don't know what to say. I'm really sorry things happened the way they did. I do think your hair looks really pretty though, Emmy." She reached over to give Emmy a hug, and Emmy forced herself to hug back. "Well, I've got to get dinner on the table," Marilyn said. "You guys take care. Say hi to Sam and Bernard." Bernard was Emmy's dad. And she was off.

Emmy's mom went into the kitchen and put the strawberries into a big bowl, which she put in the middle of the table. They looked pretty. But as Emmy marched back upstairs, she swore to herself she would not have one bite of any of those strawberries. Those strawberries could rot for all she cared.

CHAPTER 3

Monday morning. Again for a few blissful moments after
Emmy awoke, she did not think about her hair. Then
the familiar jolt of remembrance—Lizzy had chopped it.
Chopped it. It was short and she had bangs. But Josephine
had fixed it, pretty much. Emmy supposed she could
forgive Lizzy. Maybe Lizzy really was just trying to give
her a more stylish cut. Maybe she meant well, it's just
that she wasn't a professional like Josephine. Maybe she
did the best she could.

Emmy and Lizzy didn't have class together until
after lunch. For the first half of the day, no one seemed
to notice Emmy's hair. No one seemed to notice Emmy
at all, actually. And that was kind of the way it had been
so far this year. It was like she was camouflaged against

a background. And Lizzy was the opposite. She was . . . noticeable. Uncamouflage-able.

But for now Emmy had lunch to contend with. She got in the hot-lunch line and grabbed a tray. This year it suddenly seemed that the cool kids brought their lunches, and the rest got hot lunch. Last year everyone had loved hot lunch, but this year was different in so many ways.

For starters, Emmy and Lizzy used to sit together every day until the beginning of seventh grade. Sometimes just the two of them, sometimes other kids would join them. But they were always together. Then all of a sudden Emmy found herself sitting alone with her hot lunch while Lizzy sat across the room with Cadence and Sophie. With the lunches they had brought. They always seemed to be busy trading things from their lunches. They were in their own little world.

Cadence and Sophie were new to the class last year. They had both moved from the same town and had been in the same school before, so they stuck together in sixth grade. They kept pretty much to themselves, and both Emmy and Lizzy thought they were a little snobby. But all of a sudden in seventh grade Cadence and Sophie began including Lizzy in their exclusive little group while still ignoring Emmy. And now Cadence, Sophie, and Lizzy had become a threesome.

Which was surprising to Emmy because last year Sophie and Cadence had played quite a mean trick on Emmy and Lizzy in the lunchroom. It had been spaghetti and meatballs day, and both Emmy and Lizzy had gotten up to get napkins and water in the corner of the lunchroom, leaving their trays unattended. When they returned, they sat down, grabbed their forks, and dug in. But in addition to the meatballs in their spaghetti there was something truly horrifying and disgusting: eyeballs.

They were fake eyeballs, of course, but that didn't matter to Lizzy and Emmy, who both felt like throwing up. They looked up and across the room. Sophie and Cadence were doubled over laughing.

Today Emmy sat with her short hair and dipped her fish sticks in ketchup. A girl named Hannah sat across from her. Emmy and Hannah been good friends in third and fourth grade but weren't so close anymore. Hannah didn't really have any other friends to sit with, and this year they had begun sitting together at lunch. They didn't have much in common, and they didn't really talk much while eating lunch, but still it was nice not to sit alone.

Then Emmy looked over at Lizzy, Cadence, and Sophie. They seemed to be sharing something in the middle of the table and acting like it was hilarious.

I'll just go over there, Emmy thought, tired of no longer eating lunch with Lizzy, *and ask to join them. Lizzy would never say no. Lizzy's got new friends, but she's not mean.* It took Emmy a while to get up the courage. She made sure she had one fish stick left so it would be like she hadn't finished her lunch. She took a deep breath, mumbled a good-bye to Hannah, and stood up. As she approached the table, she could see what the three girls were sharing.

It was strawberry shortcake. And it looked delicious. Emmy immediately wanted some, then remembered her promise not to eat any of the "traitor strawberries," as she had come to think of them. Her mom had kept offering her some yesterday, and she had kept refusing until her mom had gotten the hint. Then her mom had given her a sympathetic look, which made Emmy want to start crying all over again.

"Hi, Lizzy," Emmy said, standing next to the table and holding her tray. Sophie and Cadence barely looked up from eating the cake, which was almost devoured.

"Excuse me?" Lizzy said, and looked directly at Emmy without smiling.

"Hi," Emmy said softly. Why had she even bothered to come over?

"Hi *who?*" Lizzy said.

"Sorry, hi, *Liz*," Emmy said.

"Hi," Lizzy said, and nothing more.

Cadence looked up. "Nice haircut," she said. Emmy couldn't tell if she was being sarcastic or not.

"Yeah, Liz has a special talent," Sophie said. "She could open her own salon."

Was she serious?

Emmy tried to smile. "Thanks for the strawberries," she said to Lizzy. She didn't mean it, but she had no idea what else to say, and she felt like she had to say something.

"What do you mean?" Lizzy asked blankly.

"Your mom brought over some of the strawberries you picked on Saturday," Emmy said.

"Oh, she did?" Lizzy said. "I didn't know that."

Lizzy picked up her fork and began working on the last of the cake. It was almost gone, which the three girls seemed to think was the funniest thing in the world.

Sophie and Cadence were laughing as hard as when they had played the eyeballs-in-the-spaghetti trick on Emmy and Lizzy last year. Only this time Lizzy was laughing with them and Emmy was on the outside. Alone.

Emmy decided to forget about sitting down. There wasn't a chair, and they certainly weren't inviting her.

"Yeah," she mumbled. "Well, see you later."

Lizzy didn't look up. Neither did Cadence or Sophie. And as Emmy walked away, they started cracking up.

Emmy went back to her table and ate her last fish stick. Her humiliation made it almost impossible to swallow.

Now she was going to have to see Lizzy again in English class next period. And, as if by some cruel twist of fate, they got paired off as editing buddies. Their teacher, Ms. Calhoun, sometimes started Monday's class with a "quick write" in which everyone had five minutes to write about something he or she had done over the weekend. Then everyone got paired off with an editing buddy, swapping papers and reading each other's work, then making corrections and notes. The editing buddies also discussed the pieces. No one knew who his or her editing buddy would be until everyone was finished writing, though.

When it was time to start writing, Emmy gripped her

pencil tightly. How could she possibly write about this weekend? She took a deep breath and started writing the first thing that came to her:

> This weekend I had a sleepover with Lizzy. She gave me a haircut. It wasn't quite what I had expected. We made purple cows, which are the best smoothys ever. Blending blueberries and bananas together is a beautiful thing. On Sunday it rained and I stayed home. And that was my weekend.

Oh well. The writing lacked her usual enthusiasm. It was stiff and clunky. But it was technically a complete paragraph.

When she learned she would be paired with Lizzy, she had the same feeling that she had when she looked in the mirror and saw her short hair. Like her stomach was melting. They swapped papers. Lizzy had written:

> Best Saturday Ever
> By Liz Draper
>
> This Saturday I spent the day with my friends and it was perfect in every way. We got up early,

but it was worth it to go strawberry picking. After we had picked enough delicious strawberries to fill Cadence's dad's trunk we went to Manhattan. First, we went shopping and I bought a gorgeous new sundress. I can't wait to wear it. And then we went to a Broadway show, which was so cool because I want to be an actress when I grow up. It was definitely the best day ever.

It was time to discuss each other's pieces. They traded papers and spent a minute reading them. Then Lizzy spoke first.

"You spelled 'smoothies' wrong," Lizzy told Emmy, tapping the word on Emmy's paper with the eraser of her pencil. "It's I-E, not Y. Other than that, it's perfect."

Emmy erased the Y and replaced it with I-E. "You think it's *perfect*?" she said. She hoped Lizzy would get what she was saying. As in, the weekend had been the exact opposite of perfect.

"I mean, it's fine," Lizzy said. "You go."

"Um, yours is good," Emmy said. What was she supposed to say? *Glad you had such a super weekend, Lizzy? Thanks for mentioning our sleepover.* "I'd put a comma after 'trunk,'" she added. "It seems like it needs a comma there."

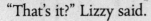

"That's it?" Lizzy said.

"Yeah," Emmy said. She guessed that really was it.

"Okay, we're done then," Lizzy said.

"I guess we are," Emmy said, and couldn't help but notice the double meaning contained in the sentence.

For the rest of class, Emmy couldn't stop thinking about that strawberry shortcake. Specifically, she thought about how the cake was made. You mixed together all these ingredients, and then when you baked it, it became something totally different—a cake. It was still all those ingredients, like sugar and flour and egg, but it had changed form.

That's what had happened to Emmy's sadness after lunch. It had somehow turned into something different— anger. Anger she felt through her whole body. She felt a little dizzy because of it, actually. And all she could think was, *I swear, Lizzy, I will find a way to let you know how angry I really am.*

CHAPTER 4

As she walked home from school, Emmy threw a little pity party for herself in her head. What a rotten day it had been. That scene at lunch with the strawberry shortcake, having to be editing buddies with Lizzy, feeling self-conscious all day about her short hair, nobody really caring enough to say anything about her haircut. But then she heard her dad's voice in her head.

"You should do something nice for yourself," her dad would sometimes say to her mom if she'd had a bad day. Her mom would do little things, like go to the gym and sit in the sauna afterward, or go for a manicure, or buy herself something she really wanted. It didn't have to be something big; even her favorite candy bar would do the trick.

Buying herself something nice suddenly seemed like a brilliant idea, and Emmy did have some money in her wallet. And her favorite little store, Zim Zam, was right on the corner of her block.

Zim Zam was like a toy store for older kids. They sold things like purses shaped like owls, mood rings, cool cards, journals, mugs, giant pencils, and other fun, quirky stuff. Whenever Emmy needed to buy anyone a present, she went to Zim Zam. The owner, Christine, was friendly with her mom and Lizzy's mom, and knew Emmy and Lizzy by name. They had all been going there forever.

The other excellent thing about Zim Zam was that there was a resident cat named Zoom. He was a sleek, handsome black cat who greeted the customers in such a friendly way that Emmy referred to him as a "puppycat." He was more like a dog than a cat.

When Emmy opened the door, the familiar bells chimed, announcing her arrival. That always made her feel special, like royalty being announced, though she knew it was just to let Christine know a new customer had entered. Still, here in this familiar place, she felt her dark mood begin to lift a little bit. And there was

Zoom, rubbing against her leg and purring loudly.

"Hi, Emmy," Christine called. She was unpacking a box of erasers shaped and colored just like real stones. "Great haircut!"

Emmy put her hand to her head. "Thanks," she smiled. It may have been her first real smile of the day. She started looking at the new animal puppets in one corner of the store, which were arranged in a rotating tower. Emmy knew she was getting too old to add to her enormous stuffed animal collection, but she couldn't help admiring these puppets. There was a sea turtle she especially liked. She put her hand inside the puppet and saw that you could control the turtle's head with your hand, sticking it out and pulling it back into its shell. *Wouldn't it be great to be a turtle and hide my head inside my shell whenever I wanted to?* she thought. *Like when I get a bad haircut, for instance. Or every day at lunch when I have to watch my old best friend sit with her new best friends.*

"Aren't those puppets great?" Christine called across the store, noticing Emmy's interest.

"They really are," Emmy replied. "I wish I had enough money for one." She dug her wallet out of her bag and checked out her cash situation. She had exactly four singles, a quarter, a nickel, and two pennies. Definitely not enough for the $19.99 puppet.

"Start saving in your piggy bank," Christine suggested. "You'll have enough soon, I bet."

"Maybe," Emmy answered. "Good idea." She spun the puppet tower around a little to see what other puppets there were, and as she did, she noticed something she had never seen before. Behind the tower was a closed door. At the same time that she saw the door, she smelled something strange. Some sort of strong, flowery smell.

Emmy had thought the toy store was just the one square room and that Christine did all her desk work at the front counter. How had she never noticed a door back here? Feeling nosy, she tried the knob and pushed the door. It swung open with a loud creak. Christine didn't look up. Then suddenly there was a face right in front of her—like three inches from her face.

"Oh!" Emmy gasped. It was as if someone had said "boo!" But no one had. Instead, there was an older woman standing just on the other side of the door. She was heavyset and had long white hair. She wore a loose-fitting blouse and a long, flowing skirt.

"What's the matter?" the woman asked kindly.

"S-Sorry," Emmy stammered. "I didn't know anyone would be in here. I was just looking at the puppets." She removed the sea turtle puppet from her hand and put it back on its post.

"Puppets are nice," the woman said. "But there are more things to see back here. Didn't you know?"

"No," Emmy said, shaking her head. "I didn't know there was anything back here." She peeked in a bit. The room was dimly lit and had a sort of red glow. It was so unlike the rest of the store that Emmy thought she must be dreaming.

"What's your name?" the woman asked.

"Emmy," she said, suddenly shy. The woman looked like the kind of fortune-teller Emmy had seen in the movies and on television. She wore giant dangly gold earrings, bangle bracelets around her wrist, and had a large mole on her cheek.

"Come in, Emmy," the woman said warmly, and Emmy slid behind the puppet tower and into the room. She felt she had left the bright, silly world of Zim Zam far behind, and as she stood in the scented room, her mood took a nosedive as she remembered her horrible day.

"What's wrong, Emmy?" asked the woman, sounding like Emmy's grandmother.

"Oh, I just had a bad day," Emmy said softly as she looked around. The room was small, but its shelves and counter were packed with all kinds of weird stuff.

There were lots of little dolls, and lots of candles in different shapes, sizes, and colors. There was a glass countertop that held bracelets, necklaces, and earrings. There were also jars of beads for making jewelry.

Emmy noticed little containers of oil and perfume, wooden sculptures of people and animals, and a tall stack of old books. Plus, there were glass goblets, crystals, drums, wooden instruments, dried gourds, shells, snakeskins, skull figurines, and blocks of wax. So many strange things!

"What happened?" the woman asked. She seemed so kind that Emmy decided to just tell the truth.

"I'm losing my best friend," Emmy whispered.

"Ah," the woman said. "And every girl needs a best friend, doesn't she?"

"I suppose so."

"This best friend of yours," the woman said. "What makes you say that you're losing her?"

"I don't know." Emmy shrugged, feeling very odd discussing this with a total stranger.

"Well, *something* must have happened," the woman pressed.

"Oh, things happened all right," Emmy said, suddenly shy no longer. "Like, she's totally treated me like I'm an annoyance all year."

The woman nodded, encouraging Emmy to continue. So Emmy did.

"And then this weekend she chopped all my hair off!" She gestured to her head.

"Wow," the woman said, still nodding. "You must really hate her."

Emmy felt strangely happy, hearing those words said aloud. She certainly hadn't said them before, or even dared think them. *Hate is a strong word,* her parents always said. She knew it would upset her mother if she told her that she *hated* Lizzy. But standing there in this weird back room with this old woman, that's exactly what she felt. She hated Lizzy.

"Yeah, I really do," Emmy said. It felt so good to admit it. Then she tried saying it out loud. "I hate her."

The woman seemed proud of Emmy for admitting

the truth. "I think I have just what you need," she said, folding her arms across her chest, standing back, and looking Emmy up and down. Then she pointed to the shelf with the small dolls on it.

Emmy stared at the shelf. She hadn't gotten a doll in a few years, since she'd outgrown them. But these didn't look like regular dolls. They were smaller and made completely of cloth, with embroidered faces and button eyes.

"They're nice," Emmy said.

"They're more than just nice," the woman said. "They'll keep you company the way a best friend does. I'm sure one would keep you better company than this former best friend of yours."

Emmy highly doubted that, but she did like them. "How much are they?" she asked the woman.

"Let's see . . ." The woman took out an old, dusty calculator from under the counter. She punched in a few numbers and then said, "With tax . . . four dollars and thirty-two cents."

Emmy gasped and held her hand to her mouth.

"What is it, Emmy?" The woman spoke to her like they were old friends.

"That's *exactly* how much I have—I just counted!" Emmy said.

"Then it was meant to be." The woman smiled. "Choose one, Emmy. Choose a little doll." She led Emmy behind the counter, where Emmy noticed a candle burning. Emmy looked at all the dolls. They were brightly colored and handmade. They were all the same shape and size, but had different colors and embroidered patterns. Without even realizing it, Emmy picked one that looked a lot like Lizzy, with yellow yarn coming out of its head that had a similar shade as Lizzy's blond hair. She took it off the shelf and looked at it closely.

"Is that the doll that is meant for you, Emmy?" the woman asked in a very serious voice.

"I think so." Emmy nodded. And as she did, she was absolutely sure of it.

"Then you must give it a name," the woman said. "And it must be the first name that comes into your mind."

Well, that was easy.

"And you must say it out loud," the woman added.

"Lizzy," Emmy whispered. She stared at the doll and said it again, a bit louder this time. "Lizzy."

CHAPTER 5

Emmy handed the woman her four dollars and thirty-two cents, stuffed the doll in her backpack, and then stood awkwardly. She knew she should just say thank you and turn to go, but she suddenly felt attached to this woman and this place. It was like a warm cozy little cave, one she wanted to curl up in.

"Well, thanks," Emmy said to the woman, shifting her weight from foot to foot.

"You're welcome, Emmy," the woman said. "Come back again, will you?"

"Sure," said Emmy. It was nice to be invited back, even if the woman just wanted to sell Emmy stuff. "And by the way, I really like the way it smells in here," she added. "What is it?"

The woman smiled knowingly. "It's lavender," she said, pointing to the burning candle.

"Cool." Emmy nodded. "Do you have some for sale? Maybe I'll come back another day and buy some."

"Certainly," the woman said. "It's a dollar a candle. And I have many different scents. Sandalwood, sage, cedar, juniper . . ."

"No, I love this one. Lavender," Emmy said.

"Lavender is calming," the woman said. "An excellent tonic for the nerves. And I see you could use such a thing."

Emmy was embarrassed. A tonic for the nerves. Was it that obvious what a mess she was? Apparently, yes.

The woman reached under the counter and pulled out a candle. "For you, Emmy," she said. "No charge. But you must light this yourself in order for its calming properties to take effect."

"Wow, thank you," Emmy said as she reached out and took the candle. What a sweet thing for the woman to do. If, on a scale of one to ten, today had been a two, the woman had just turned it into a three. "Thank you very much."

"You're very welcome," the woman said.

Emmy liked being in the little room but realized she

couldn't stay there forever. It was time to say good-bye to the woman and go home. "Well, thanks," she said again.

"You're very welcome," the woman repeated.

Emmy turned to go, and as she approached the door, the woman said loudly and sharply, "Emmy!"

Emmy spun around, startled. Something had really changed in the woman's voice.

"Close the door behind you," the woman said evenly.

"No problem," Emmy said, still a little shaken. She closed the door behind her and was suddenly back in Zim Zam, with all its playful, plastic stuff. The total opposite of what was in the other room.

Emmy crossed the store, thinking that she'd ask Christine about the little room, and how long it had been there, and why she had never seen this little store within the store before. But Christine was busy with a customer and Emmy headed out, the door jangling behind her. Zoom, seeming freaked out, stared at her as she left.

Even though she'd spent plenty of time at Zim Zam and in the newly discovered back room, Emmy still had a couple of hours to finish her homework before dinner.

She sat at her desk and unpacked her backpack, taking out her books and notebooks, the doll, and the candle. She spread them all on her desk.

Maybe I'll do something nice for myself, she thought, *and light the candle. A tonic to calm my nerves after my horrible day.* She loved the sound of that: *A tonic to calm my nerves.* It sounded like magic. But she didn't have a little holder or plate for it, and she didn't want to get wax all over her desk. She went into Sam's room without knocking. He didn't seem to care.

"Do you have a little plate or container?" she asked her brother. "I need something to put this on." She showed him the candle.

"What?" Sam asked. He was deeply involved in putting the finishing touches on a model dinosaur in a corner of his room.

"A little plate or container," Emmy said.

"Um, sure. There's a little ceramic tile I made, over there." He pointed to his nightstand.

"That'll do," Emmy said. "Thanks." She grabbed the hand-painted tile and went back into her room. But Sam followed her. Emmy spun around as Sam entered.

"What do you want?" she asked him, a bit

impatiently. She wanted to get started with the candle.

"I was just wondering if I could light the candle," he said. "Mom and Dad let me light candles on your birthday cake now because I know how to be safe with matches."

"Sorry," Emmy said. "I have to light it myself. That's the whole idea. It's a magic candle. But you could go downstairs and get the matches for me, though. Would you?" Sam seemed happy to be given this task and left the room. When he came back up, he handed her the matches.

"Thanks," Emmy said to her brother. "You can stay here while I light it if you want."

"Okay," Sam said, pleased.

Emmy struck a match carefully and held it to the wick. Right away, the candle began filling the room with the now-familiar lavender scent. She and Sam stared at it for a minute, mesmerized by its steady glow, until Emmy broke the silence and told Sam that she had to start her homework.

Emmy breathed deeply as she started her Spanish homework. The class was studying food words, and the assignment was to make up a menu for her own restaurant. As she thought about the foods she'd serve at her restaurant, Casa de Emmy, she absentmindedly twirled the doll on the desk. It felt very satisfying to spin it around and around.

Hamburguesas, she wrote on her menu. *Papas fritas.* Yum, hamburgers and fries. She was hungry for dinner already. Just then, her mom knocked on her half-open door.

"Hi, honey. What's that smell?" her mom asked. "I could smell it from downstairs."

"Guess." Emmy smiled, looking at the candle.

"First, it's nice to see you smile," her mom said. "I haven't seen that in a few days. Second, hmm, I don't know exactly what the scent is. Something floral."

"You're on the right track," Emmy said. Her mom closed her eyes and took a deep breath.

"Lavender?" she guessed.

"Bingo!" Emmy said and gestured to the candle. "It's supposed to be a tonic for my nerves."

"It's pretty," her mom said. "But from now on, I'm going to have to insist that you only burn candles downstairs, when your father or I are around. I'm not comfortable with you burning candles up here alone."

Emmy nodded and blew out the candle. She understood her mother's point.

Her mother continued. "Where'd you get it?" she asked.

"Zim Zam," Emmy said.

"They sell candles there?" her mom asked. "I didn't realize that. I thought it was more like just toys."

"They opened this new section of the store," Emmy said.

"What do you mean?" her mom asked, raising her eyebrows.

"There's, like, this little back room where there's other stuff," Emmy explained vaguely.

"Hmm," her mom said. "I never noticed that. What else did you get? This little doll?" Her mom pointed.

"Yeah," Emmy said. "It cost four dollars and thirty two cents, and that's exactly how much I had. So it was meant to be."

"Then how did you buy the candle?" her mom asked.

"Oh, the lady there was really nice, and she gave it to me."

"She gave it to you?" her mom asked, looking surprised. Emmy hoped her mother wasn't going to make her give it back. She realized that it was kind of odd to take a gift from a stranger, and that her mom probably wouldn't like it. But her mom let the matter drop, and picked up the doll and examined it. "Well, the doll's interesting," she said. "Pretty." She placed it back on the desk.

"Thanks," Emmy said. She twirled it around again on the desk. It spun easily, like a toy top. Just like the candle, it felt kind of soothing.

Another day with short hair, Emmy thought as she woke the next morning. She had to admit she was feeling slightly better than she had during the previous days. Maybe she was getting used to the haircut. Maybe it wasn't so bad after all. And it would grow back. Eventually. *This too shall pass,* her dad liked to say.

Her bedroom still smelled slightly of lavender from yesterday. *Maybe it's working,* Emmy thought. *Maybe it is a tonic for my nerves.* She went downstairs in her pajamas and for the first time wasn't shocked by her own reflection when she passed herself in the mirror.

Walking to school, though, she felt the familiar

pangs of sadness. She and Lizzy used to walk together every morning, and now she walked alone. She looked around for Lizzy. For the past few months, they'd been walking to school separately, but if they ran into each other, they would join up and walk together. But there was no sign of her today.

Lunchtime came quickly enough. On her way to lunch, she picked up her pace so she could get in line early for the hot lunch, before it got too long. The sooner she got in line, she figured, the sooner she'd be eating lunch. She wasn't exactly running, but walking as fast as one could without breaking into a run. As she cruised down the hall, two boys stood at their lockers, watching her.

"You better hurry up!" one of them said sarcastically. "It might be all gone by the time you get there!"

Ugh. Emmy had forgotten it so wasn't cool to rush through the halls . . . especially for the school lunch.

There was a silver lining, though. She did get in line early. And today was pizza day, and the pizza was extra cheesy and delicious. She smiled at Hannah as she sat down. As she took her second bite, she realized she hadn't even looked over at the table where Lizzy usually sat with Cadence and Sophie. Maybe she really was starting to adjust to the new reality of life without her best friend. She used to get a stomachache every time she entered the lunchroom, and now she was eating somewhat happily and forgetting to notice Lizzy's table.

But she did look over eventually, of course, and saw Cadence and Sophie, but no Lizzy. Once she'd finished her pizza, she said good-bye to Hannah and walked slowly past the table holding her empty tray. She strained to listen to their conversation.

"Gross!" Cadence was saying.

"I know, right?" Sophie responded.

"Poor Liz," Cadence said.

Emmy couldn't help herself. She turned to them. "What's the matter with Lizzy, I mean Liz?" she asked.

Cadence and Sophie looked up. They seemed irritated by the interruption.

"Liz was up all night kissing the porcelain god," Cadence said with a straight face.

Emmy had no idea what she was talking about. Cadence and Sophie began to giggle.

Sophie chimed in. "Liz was up all night tossing her

cookies," she added. Emmy was more confused than before.

Sophie and Cadence seemed to think it was quite funny that Emmy wasn't following the conversation. They laughed harder.

"She lost her lunch," Sophie added. "And dinner!"

"Oh," Emmy said. She felt so stupid as she realized Lizzy had been throwing up. At first she felt bad for Lizzy. Throwing up was the worst! Then she felt a small twinge of pleasure. Throwing up *was* the worst, and didn't Lizzy deserve to feel *terrible* for a little while?

"Oh. That's the worst," Emmy said after a pause.

"I know, right?" Cadence said. "I got a text from her this morning. She said she felt like she was spinning around on a crazy-fast merry-go-round all night. But I think she's better now."

"That's good," Emmy said, not really meaning it. *Maybe she ate too many of those traitor strawberries,* she thought. *Serves her right.*

CHAPTER 6

After school that day Sam was sitting on the steps as Emmy tossed her bag down and went into the kitchen for a snack. Sam wasn't so bad, as far as little brothers went. But he did have two major flaws. One, he constantly wanted to be included in everything Emmy did. Two, he was always pawing through Emmy's things. Usually, it seemed, he was in search of sweets, which Emmy liked to keep stashed in her bag. (Their mom was a little too concerned about limiting their sugar intake, so what was Emmy supposed to do?)

Pawing through Emmy's bag was exactly what Sam was doing after school that day as he sat on the steps, and he hit the jackpot. Gummy bears! Emmy saw the flash of the wrapper as she came back into the room, and Sam leapt quickly up the stairs.

"Um, *hello?*" Emmy called after her brother.

Sam turned around innocently. "Hello," he said, as if Emmy hadn't been being sarcastic with her "hello."

"What did you steal from my bag?" Emmy snapped.

"Nothing," Sam said, hiding both hands behind his back. He was such a bad liar.

"Give it," Emmy said, lunging up the steps.

Sam had a "busted!" look on his face as he held out the package of gummy bears and Emmy grabbed it. But one hand was still behind his back.

Emmy sighed impatiently. "Do you really think I don't realize you have something else in your other hand?"

Poor Sam looked totally defeated as he held out his other hand, which gripped the little doll Emmy had bought the day before. Suddenly Emmy was more than mildly annoyed, she was furious. Which was strange because she'd barely given the doll any thought since yesterday. When she'd cleared her desk off before school, she'd stuffed it in her backpack, but didn't even remember that it had been in there all day. Suddenly she felt very attached to it.

As quickly as it had taken Emmy's reaction to shift

from annoyed to furious, Sam's expression changed from guilty to nasty, and he threw the doll as hard as he could all the way down the staircase, then ran into his room and slammed the door. Emmy scrambled down the stairs to retrieve the doll, grateful that it was made of cloth and therefore not breakable. *Little brothers can be such a royal pain,* she thought as she stuffed the doll back into the front pocket of her backpack.

Every day before school, if it wasn't raining or freezing cold, kids liked to hang out in the yard before the bell rang. Of course, when Lizzy and Emmy used to walk to school together, they'd hang out there too, joining in a game other kids were playing or sometimes just talking to each other. Now Emmy faced this before-school scene alone, and Lizzy hung out with Sophie and Cadence. They were always giggling and looking as if they were having just the greatest time ever enjoying some grand private joke.

But as she approached the school yard the next morning, something looked different, even from a distance. There were lots of kids standing around Lizzy, not just Sophie and Cadence. Lizzy definitely seemed to be the center of everyone's attention. And they were all focused on something near the ground.

As Emmy got closer, she saw that one of Lizzy's legs was thick and white. Oh, wait, that would be a cast, Emmy realized. And Lizzy was standing with crutches.

It was always such a big deal when someone showed up at school with a cast, as if he or she had been away at war and lived to come home and tell the tale. Rumors quickly circulated—*The bone in his arm was sticking right through the skin! She had to be taken in an ambulance to the emergency room!*—and the kid with the cast usually appeared to enjoy the attention.

And Lizzy, it seemed, was no exception. She was talking and laughing, gesturing dramatically to the crowd.

Emmy felt a rush of sympathy and concern for Lizzy. Forget about the extra attention, breaking a bone couldn't have been fun. It had to have really hurt. Emmy wanted to know what had happened, so she approached the crowd. But she could barely get near Lizzy with so many kids swarmed around her.

Lizzy had managed to accommodate her cast and still look great in her outfit. She barely looked awkward at all. She was wearing a pair of leggings with the one leg rolled way up to show the whole cast, which was bright white and clean. When Emmy took a closer look, she saw that there were thin pencil marks on it dividing the cast into seven stripes.

As if reading Emmy's mind, Cadence asked, "So what are those pencil marks for?"

Lizzy's face lit up as she dug into her backpack and pulled out a package of thin permanent markers in every color of the rainbow. "My mom had a great idea," Lizzy announced to the crowd. "When everyone signs the cast, they can use a different color in a different section. So when everyone's finished signing, my cast will look like a big handwritten rainbow. The more people who sign it, the better!" Kids nodded and oohed and ahhed appreciatively as the bell rang. And besides Sophie and Cadence, several boys were scrambling to help Lizzy inside to start the school day. It was as if she had her own private staff of butlers.

Emmy was glad her first few classes weren't with Lizzy. She already needed a break from *The Lizzy Show* after the scene in the playground. *Funny how no one even noticed my haircut*, she thought, *and yet they can't take their eyes off Lizzy's cast.* She dreaded lunch and the scene she was sure she would see in the cafeteria—kids lining up to sign Lizzy's cast. She wasn't too far off base, either. There wasn't exactly a line, but there was a small crowd around Lizzy's table during the entire lunch period. Kids were taking turns trying to walk with her crutches. Emmy tried to focus on her grilled cheese and tomato soup. "Comfort food," her mom would have called it. But it wasn't much comfort at all.

As usual, she and Lizzy had English together after lunch. They'd been reading haiku, and Ms. Calhoun explained that now it was time to try writing their own. A haiku has three lines. The first has five syllables, the second has seven syllables, and the third has five syllables. It was fun to try to fit the syllables into the correct pattern. At the end of class, anyone who wanted to could read his or her haiku to the group. Emmy struggled to transport herself to a different time and place to write about, and decided on the Fourth of July, which, coincidentally, was the last time she and Lizzy had really had fun together. They'd walked with their families to the river and watched fireworks go off over the Manhattan skyline.

FIREWORKS

Pop, bam, sizzle, boom
Colors lighting up the dark
Independence Day

Emmy was pretty pleased with her haiku, but when Ms. Calhoun invited students to read their work to the group, she felt shy and didn't raise her hand. Lizzy did, though, and when called on, slowly struggled to get to her feet and reach her crutches so she could stand in front of the class.

"It's okay, Lizzy," Ms. Calhoun said. "You can read from your desk." Lizzy seemed disappointed about this, but took a dramatic breath before she began reading:

PAIN
Sharp, stabbing zinger!
Pain rushes through me and I
Can't even breathe right

"Wow, very nice, Lizzy," Ms. Calhoun said. "I assume this was about your recent experience of breaking your leg?" Everyone laughed. Except Emmy. Because the truth was, Lizzy's haiku described Emmy's hurt feelings just perfectly.

The day wore on and each time Emmy saw Lizzy, she was surrounded by a team of helpers. And as promised, her cast was slowly becoming a handwritten rainbow. Emmy wondered if Lizzy would ask her to sign it. But by the end of the day Lizzy hadn't even glanced in Emmy's direction. It was as if Emmy didn't exist.

Once again Emmy felt her sadness harden into anger as she walked home alone. She even felt a little glad that Lizzy had broken her leg. No more strawberry picking, and it would definitely put a damper on any costume she had planned with Cadence and Sophie. What kind of costume could incorporate a big clunky cast? *Never mind,* Emmy thought bitterly, *Lizzy will think of some fabulous way to make it work. And everyone will feel so sorry for poor Lizzy that she'll win first prize.*

Then suddenly Emmy emerged from these thoughts and realized she had never found out how Lizzy had broken her leg.

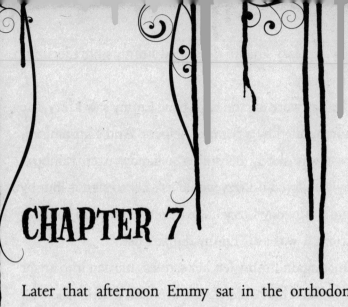

CHAPTER 7

Later that afternoon Emmy sat in the orthodontist's waiting room. Dr. Costa's office was just a block away from her house, so her parents had started letting her go to routine appointments like this one by herself. Today she was just going to have her clear braces tightened, which was a quick and painless procedure. The discomfort would come in the next few days, when her whole mouth would be sore from the tightening.

If only braces were as cool as a broken leg, she thought, leafing through a women's fashion magazine in the waiting room. Page after page of models stared back at her, looking about as far from human as aliens. One wore a dress that looked like it was made of aluminum foil; another had a face painted like a leopard. She didn't usually read these kinds of magazines but was strangely drawn to the images. It was sort of impossible to look away. "Fashion" was a word she had heard spoken by Lizzy all too often lately, and it seemed like something Emmy needed to learn a thing or two about. She didn't even like shopping, though, so how would she ever change her look from kid to tween?

It felt like it was taking a long time for her name to be called. She flipped a page and saw a model with black nail polish on. Emmy herself had only ever painted her nails pink or red, but come to think of it, she'd seen a few girls at school with darker colors on their nails, like deep blue or purple. She and Lizzy used to give each other manicures and pedicures using their mothers' nail polish, which was the usual variety of pinks and reds.

Maybe it would be cool to do something new, Emmy thought. *The black seems kind of cool.* And then a thought popped into her head. It was a thought she wasn't proud of, but there it was nonetheless.

Maybe Lizzy would think it was cool.

After all, painting her nails black was a risk Lizzy hadn't taken, and this time Emmy could be the one to show Lizzy a thing or two about what looked cool.

Emmy kept thinking about Lizzy telling her she needed to update her look. Well, consider it updated.

On her way home Emmy stopped at the drugstore and examined her choices. She was surprised by how many different colors there were on display. She'd never thought much about nail polish, actually, and now realized there were people whose job it was to name the colors. What a cool job! Satin Slipper. Peony. Candy-Apple Red. And finally, Midnight, which was the one she grabbed, brought to the counter, and paid for.

When she got home, Emmy emptied her backpack out onto her desk as usual. Her books, her notebooks, her nail polish, her pens and pencils, and her little doll. She picked up the bottle of nail polish and stared at it. Then, as suddenly as she'd gotten the idea to paint her fingernails black, she realized how crazy it was. She imagined Lizzy's table at lunch with Sophie and Cadence and their snarky laughter. She remembered the model in the magazine and how tall and elegant she was, and the outrageous clothes she was wearing. Emmy was neither tall nor elegant and owned nothing that could even remotely be considered outrageous. She sighed. Who did she think she was fooling?

Okay, it's only nail polish, she thought, trying to talk herself down. Then she saw the doll out of the corner of her eye. She was not as into it—or the lavender candle—as she had been earlier in the week. In fact, looking at it now, she wondered what made her buy the silly little doll. But then she had an idea for a new use for it. *Maybe I'll just start by testing out the black nail polish on the doll,* she thought. *A practice run.* She reached for the doll and set it in front of her. She gave the small glass bottle a good shake and twisted open the cap. Then she carefully, delicately applied the black lacquer to the tips of the doll's tiny fingers. She had to really focus because the fingertips were so small, but she was able to dab a dot of the enamel on each of the doll's fingertips.

When she had finished, she tilted her chair back and examined her work. *Interesting,* she thought. *It looks kind of cool.* Now that she saw it on the doll, she decided to paint her own nails. Once she'd finished and her nails had dried, she started on her math homework, which was a breeze. Soon her dad called her downstairs for dinner.

Like lunch, dinner was always a bright spot in Emmy's day. Her parents had a rule that the four of them sit down together each night, no matter how busy they all were. Her dad liked to do something called "highs and lows," which was when everyone went around the table and said the worst and best parts of their day. Emmy didn't even have to think about her low.

"My low kind of lasted all day," she admitted. Her mom gave her a sympathetic look, and her dad raised his eyebrows. Sam seemed involved with his meat loaf.

"Do tell," her dad said.

"Lizzy broke her leg," Emmy told her parents, then realized by the looks on their faces that they already knew. Of course they did; Lizzy's mom would have told them. "And she was the center of attention all day, like no one had ever seen a cast before. Everyone was falling all over themselves trying to help her."

Her mom put down her fork. "I don't suppose she asked you for any help," she said gently.

"That's right," Emmy said. "She basically ignored me all day. Then in English she wrote this really overly dramatic haiku that she read to the class. I think she loves the attention."

Her parents were silent.

"She's such a drama queen!" Emmy exclaimed as tears sprung to her eyes. She didn't even feel like finishing her meat loaf, which was one of her favorite meals.

"Oh, honey," her mom said. "That sounds really hard." Her dad nodded in agreement.

"Did your day have a high point?" her dad asked. Emmy had to think hard to find something good to say.

"My math homework was really easy," she said reluctantly.

"That's great," her mom said. "You've been doing really well in math this year. Hey, I have an idea. Why don't you do something nice for yourself tonight? Since you've finished your homework, why don't I set up the TV in your room and you can watch a movie before you go to sleep?"

Emmy had to admit that sounded pretty good.

"Can I watch it too?" Sam asked.

"For a while," Emmy said.

Sam smiled, pleased. "Hey, cool nails," he said to his sister.

"Yeah, honey," their mom added. "That's a bold new look for you."

"Thanks," Emmy said, holding out her fingers and admiring them.

Later, as she got under the covers and her mom

popped in a DVD, Emmy felt like she could stay in bed forever. In fact, it felt so good to be in bed that she found herself nodding off and falling asleep before the movie even really got going.

She had crazy dreams, bits and pieces of weirdness that she wouldn't even be able to remember—much less describe—when she woke up. But one part she would remember. It was about Lizzy.

Lizzy, sitting at her kitchen table, a bowl of strawberries next to her and a bunch of rainbow-colored permanent markers strewn about. She didn't look like her usual carefree self. She looked horrible—terribly unhappy. She clutched a bottle of black nail polish reluctantly but so tightly that her knuckles had turned white.

Slowly, Lizzy pried open the bottle and began painting her thumbnail black. The way she was acting, it was as if someone was making her do it, as if she was being forced to proceed but was trying to fight it. Once she had applied a few strokes, Lizzy held out her thumbnail and examined it, frowning. She repeated this procedure for each of her ten nails and when she was finished, she held out her hands and grimaced.

"What, you don't like it?" Emmy asked, looking on. She felt wild and cruel. "I think it looks cool."

Emmy woke up with a start and tried to fit together the pieces of her dream. Too often, remembering her dreams was like holding a handful of dry sand—when she tried, the sand just slowly slipped through her fingers. All she could remember about her dream was that it was about Lizzy, and that Lizzy was very unhappy about her fingernails. But Emmy remembered very clearly what she had said to Lizzy at the end of the dream:

What, you don't like it? I think it looks cool.

Those were the very words Lizzy had said to her after the horrible haircut. Emmy remembered feeling very happy in the dream . . . happy about Lizzy's unhappiness. She wasn't proud of this feeling, but there it was. *Maybe that's why I had the dream,* she figured. *I'm wishing bad things on Lizzy.* She felt bad about that, too, but couldn't help it.

There was something else she couldn't help doing. Something she had never done before. She got out of bed and peered out her window and into Lizzy's room, breaking their rule against spying on each other. Lizzy seemed to be getting ready for school, just like Emmy. She was taking books off her desk and putting them in her backpack. She definitely didn't see Emmy, which was how Emmy wanted it. *Forget about the no-spying rule,* she thought. *She's been so horrible to me she deserves it.*

Later that day Emmy sat with Hannah at lunch like usual, and like usual she felt lonely. She didn't eat much. Her mouth was starting to feel sore from her braces being tightened yesterday. She looked over at Lizzy's table. Sophie and Cadence were looking at Lizzy's hands and laughing. Lizzy seemed embarrassed and looked like she was trying to hide her hands. What was going on? Emmy had to know. She got up to bus her tray and walked slowly past their table, glad for once to be ignored by them.

"It's just really not your color," Sophie was saying to Lizzy with a note of disdain in her voice. "What were you even thinking?"

"I honestly don't know," Lizzy answered. "I got in a really weird mood."

"So you went out and bought black nail polish?" Cadence asked, incredulous.

"Um, no," Lizzy muttered. "I used a black Sharpie."

Then Emmy got a glimpse of the focus of the conversation: Lizzy's fingernails. They were black. It was a very dramatic look against her pale skin.

And Lizzy also looked sort of horrible, actually, like she hadn't been sleeping. For a minute Emmy felt bad for her. She knew how it felt to be spoken to that way. And she really missed Lizzy. So when she saw Lizzy in the hall a few minutes later as they both headed to English class, she gave Lizzy a gentle nudge and slowed down to her pace. Lizzy walked pretty slowly with the crutches, and today Sophie and Cadence weren't carrying her bags or helping her. Would they really be ignoring her just because she had black fingernails?

"How are you?" Emmy asked, trying to sound casual. But Lizzy didn't hear her. She seemed distracted.

Emmy repeated herself. "How are you?" she asked Lizzy a little louder this time. Lizzy slowly looked her way, a totally blank expression on her face.

"Hell-oooo?" Emmy waved her hand in front of Lizzy's face. "Earth to Lizzy, oops, I mean Liz," she said. She wanted Lizzy to notice her fingernails.

"How crazy is it that we both decided to try black nail

polish on the same day?" Emmy asked Lizzy, laughing nervously.

But Lizzy still ignored her as she walked into the classroom.

So Lizzy didn't see the look on Emmy's face as her expression of hurt and anger at being ignored suddenly melted into shock as she began to make the connection between yesterday and today.

The buying of the black nail polish, the applying of the black nail polish to the little doll, the dream in which Lizzy was putting on the black nail polish as if being forced.

It's like whatever happens to the doll, happens to Lizzy, Emmy thought.

The next thing she thought was that she was crazy for thinking such a ridiculous thing. As she sat down in her usual seat behind Lizzy, she took her notebook and English textbook out of her backpack and listened to the chatter around her.

"I broke my leg in third grade," a boy named Max was saying to Lizzy.

"How'd you do it?" Lizzy asked Max.

"Skiing in Vermont," Max said. "How did you break yours?"

"I fell down the stairs," Lizzy answered, rolling her eyes. "I'm such a klutz," she added.

Whatever happens to the doll does happen to Lizzy, Emmy thought again. And this time the thought was like a bomb exploding inside her head. She couldn't take a full breath.

Spinning the doll around on my desk made Lizzy throw up. Sam threw the doll down the stairs, and she broke her leg. I painted the doll's fingernails with black nail polish and Lizzy did the same to her fingernails.

She'd forgotten until this moment that the woman in the shop had told her to give the doll a name, and Emmy had said the first name that popped into her mind: Lizzy.

What a doll, she thought, remembering the phrase her grandmother sometimes used when someone went out of their way to be nice. But in Emmy's mind, at this moment, the phrase sounded nothing like her grandmother's expression. It sounded sinister. It was indeed a special kind of doll that could do special kinds of things.

And then one thought reverberated in Emmy's head as she directed it like an invisible laser beam right at Lizzy's sassy and stupid short blond haircut:

You'll be sorry for what you've done to me, Lizzy Draper. You'll be sorry for what you've done.

CHAPTER 8

On the walk home Emmy thought about Sophie and Cadence. Besides being angry with Lizzy, she realized just how angry she was with Lizzy's new best friends, too. It seemed like they had influenced Lizzy to not be friends with Emmy—that they had swooped down and plucked Lizzy away from the little nest of friendship she and Emmy had once shared, like she had seen birds of prey do on the nature channel. Everything had been going fine until Lizzy had become friends with them, at which point she had totally blown Emmy off.

I just want things to be the way they were, Emmy thought. *I just want it to be me and Lizzy, best friends, no one else. Lizzy's the only friend I need, and I want to be the only friend she* needs.

And now, astonishingly, there seemed to be a way to

make anything happen, as far as Lizzy was concerned. How could this little doll have such magical powers? Emmy *knew* there had been something very strange about that woman in the back room at Zim Zam.

She also knew this: Sophie and Cadence were mean, and so it would be easy to turn them against Lizzy. It was just a matter of how. Then Emmy could come to Lizzy's rescue and be her friend again. The only friend she needed.

And tonight was the perfect night to begin. It was Thursday night and the beginning of a long weekend. She'd overheard Lizzy in the hall telling someone she was having a sleepover party at her house that night, with Sophie and Cadence. The sting of what had happened at one of Lizzy's sleepovers last weekend, and not being invited to this one that would be going on just a few yards from her own room, gave way to a different feeling, and a plan took shape in Emmy's head.

After dinner that night Emmy stuck her head into Sam's room. He was at his desk, drawing.

"Hi!" she said, just a little more friendly and cheerful than the usual way she spoke to him. He looked up, surprised and, it seemed, more than a little pleased.

"Hi," he said. "What're you doing?"

"I came to see if you wanted to play," she said.

Sam's face lit up. "Sure. Let's play zoo," he suggested, referring to a game they had played with their stuffed animals when they were younger. Sam dutifully began organizing the huge pile of stuffed animals as if they lived in a zoo.

"Actually, I have another special toy to play with," Emmy told Sam.

"A stuffed animal?" Sam asked.

"Not really. It's a doll," Emmy said. Sam wrinkled his nose.

"No, it's that new doll. You know, the little one? It's a cool game, I promise," Emmy added quickly, trying to sell Sam on the idea of playing with it. "Look." She ran into her room, grabbed the doll, and rushed back into Sam's room, wiggling it around in the air.

"Okay," Sam said. "What's the game?"

"Um, I don't have a name for it," Emmy began, "But let's play in my room, okay?" Sam nodded a bit reluctantly but grabbed a few of his favorite stuffed animals and then followed Emmy into her room. And that's when Emmy took a good look out her window . . . right into Lizzy's room.

Lizzy, Sophie, and Cadence were all there. A big-screen television sat in the corner of her room. Emmy wondered if Lizzy's parents had bought it for their darling, popular Liz as a get-well-soon present, or if they were just allowing her to borrow one from another room for her big sleepover with her real best friends.

From what Emmy could see, the three girls were gearing up to watch television, play video games, and eat junk food, which was available in huge amounts. Three sleeping bags were spread out in front of the television. Emmy could feel the expression on her face morph into a scowl as she remembered all the times *she* had spread out her sleeping bag on Lizzy's floor.

Emmy turned her attention back to Sam. "Look what I can do." Emmy threw the doll up high and caught it. Sam smiled, impressed.

"Now you try," Emmy said, tossing the doll to Sam and then peering out her window again. Sam gladly accepted the challenge and began throwing the doll up and catching it. A few times he threw it so high that the doll hit the ceiling. And a few times Sam missed and the doll landed with a thud on the hardwood floor.

As Sam tossed, threw, and twisted the little doll

around, Emmy continued to watch what was happening in Lizzy's room. The girls were sprawled out and relaxed on their sleeping bags, but then something crazy started happening. Lizzy sprang up and began jumping up and down as high as she could, cast and all. She jumped and jumped like she was on a pogo stick, her cast banging on the floor.

Cadence's body language suggested that she was telling Lizzy to sit down, and Lizzy sat down sheepishly. But about five seconds later she started jumping again. A few times she lost her balance and fell hard on the ground. Now Sophie and Cadence were staring at her as if she'd completely lost her mind.

Emmy turned her attention back to Sam, who had started making the doll do a funny little dance.

"What else can you make it do?" Emmy prodded her brother, who had begun making a stuffed monkey stand on its head. He shrugged. He seemed to be losing interest in playing with the doll and was more interested in his animals. Emmy had to do something.

"How about making the doll stand on its head like your monkey?" Emmy asked. She knew it was a lame little game, but Sam was just a little boy and he seemed happy to have the company and to please Emmy.

"Yeah!" Sam said, and began balancing the doll on its head, where it stayed for a few moments before eventually falling over.

Time to look out the window again, Emmy thought with glee.

And what a scene it was. First Lizzy was doing a weird little dance, her arms and legs flailing about as though she were a puppet on a string. And then, without a pause, she went straight into a headstand, balancing awhile before falling and knocking over a bowl of potato chips with her big cast. The chips landed all over the floor and in the sleeping bags.

Sophie got up to clean up the chips, looking extremely put out. *Maybe they won't be able to sleep with all the crumbs in their sleeping bags,* Emmy thought. *Oh well. Too bad.*

And then Lizzy went right into another headstand, her rainbow cast sticking high up in the air. Sophie and Cadence stared at her, their mouths wide open in shock. Then Cadence whispered something to Sophie and they both laughed.

After her second headstand, Lizzy went back to her place on the bed, like she didn't know what had come over her all of a sudden. Like someone else had taken over her body. She sat down for a minute and looked at the television screen.

Oh, no, thought Emmy. *I'm not done with you yet.*

Emmy turned around. "My turn!" she crowed to Sam. By now she had positioned herself in such a way that she could see into Lizzy's window and play with Sam at the same time. "Look what I can do with it." She threw the doll against the wall so hard that it bounced off and landed with a loud *plunk* on the floor. Emmy picked it up and did it again as Sam laughed and laughed. This was the most fun Emmy could remember having with her brother.

Then, like a jack-in-the-box, Lizzy popped off the couch and ran straight into the wall, hard. Then she collapsed on the floor in a heap.

Sophie hit a button on the remote control, pausing whatever it was they were watching. Sophie and Cadence continued to look annoyed, and they looked like they were yelling at her. Emmy could just imagine their snobby voices: *Would you stop! Seriously, what is your problem?* But Lizzy ran into the wall again and again. Depending on how Emmy threw the doll, sometimes Lizzy would slide feet first, sometimes she'd slam her shoulder into the wall. Each time, she hit the wall so hard that she'd fall down. But each time, she'd get up and do it again. She looked like a little kid who wasn't getting enough attention and had resorted to doing crazy tricks.

Finally, she stopped and sat there on the floor, confused. She looked dazed. *More specifically,* Emmy thought, *she looks like a cartoon character who has just hit its head. Stars and swirls might as well be circling above her.* For a split second Emmy worried that maybe she went a little too far. After all, what if she had given Lizzy a concussion? But then Emmy shoved the thought out of her head. Lizzy was just getting what she deserved, Emmy figured.

Then Lizzy's mom entered the room. She looked concerned and more than a little perplexed. She bent down next to Lizzy, and Cadence and Sophie looked like they were explaining something to her. They still looked totally annoyed, but also a little scared.

How's your fabulous sleepover going now? Emmy asked Lizzy in her head. *Guess it's not going exactly the way you'd planned. Guess you hadn't planned on being a total spaz.*

Lizzy sat up straight and looked like she was trying

to collect herself. Then Emmy saw Cadence and Sophie rolling up their sleeping bags and putting on their backpacks. They walked slowly out of the room as Lizzy's mom gently tried to put Lizzy in bed and tuck her in under the covers. She must have thought she had a fever or something. She must have thought she was delirious.

And that seemed to be the end of Lizzy's sleepover party. Emmy laughed out loud, forgetting that Sam was still in the room. She couldn't help herself. It was probably the last time Cadence and Sophie would ever talk to Lizzy again.

Emmy went to sleep that night unable to stop herself from feeling wildly pleased by her actions with the little doll. What a fool Lizzy had made of herself at her own sleepover party!

The next morning Emmy felt more energetic than she had in a long time. She enjoyed her weekend. She was in such a good mood she offered to help her mom do the grocery shopping and her dad sort the recycling. She also helped Sam with his homework, which pleased her parents to no end. All the while she kept the doll on her desk. She was just waiting for inspiration. What else could she do to Lizzy with this magic little doll?

Monday morning finally rolled around and for once she found herself not dreading going to school. As she approached the school building, she noticed Lizzy making her way through the front door on her crutches . . . alone. Where was her usual entourage? They were nowhere to be seen.

Now she'll know what it's like to feel ignored. Emmy thought, barely able to keep the smile off her face. At lunch Emmy glanced over at Lizzy's usual spot with Sophie and Cadence, but Lizzy wasn't there. Emmy scanned the lunchroom, trying to find her. She finally saw her eating alone at a table near the corner. She looked miserable. As Emmy got up to bus her tray, she walked slowly by Sophie and Cadence. She could hear their conversation clearly. Being invisible had its benefits.

"Whatever," Sophie was saying. "If she wants to be weird, let her be weird with other people. She didn't need to ruin my night."

"I know, right?" Cadence replied. "She was acting like she'd just escaped from the loony bin." This made both girls crack up.

Emmy continued walking with her tray and, as she exited the lunchroom, took a backward glance at Lizzy, alone in the corner, her crutches propped up on the wall next to her. For a moment she felt bad for her and paused as she considered going over to Lizzy and talking to her. Then she remembered what a totally bad friend Lizzy had been to her. *Let her come to me,* Emmy thought as she turned her back and walked out of the cafeteria.

After school, sitting at her kitchen table, Emmy made herself a snack of crackers and peanut butter. Happily munching away, Emmy replayed the day's events in her mind and relished the idea of Lizzy's rapidly dwindling popularity. *Could Lizzy even get more miserable?* Emmy wondered. *Oh, yes. Yes she could.*

Emmy went to her room and picked up the doll from her desk, stroking its long yarn hair. She looked out her window into Lizzy's room, but her old friend wasn't there.

"Don't you think it's about time for a makeover?" Emmy asked out loud, addressing the doll. "I have a vision."

She reached across the desk for her scissors and held them out, pointing them at the doll like a magic wand.

Then Emmy slowly, methodically cut the doll's hair off, in as random a pattern as possible. There were pieces sticking out every which way. It took a few minutes to snip all that yarn off. When she had finished, she held the doll up and admired her work.

Emmy looked at the doll as if it had spoken to her. "What, you don't like it?" she asked the doll innocently. The doll's button eyes stared back vacantly.

Emmy's voice had two layers: it was warm on the surface but cold as ice underneath. "I think it looks cool."

CHAPTER 9

As she got dressed for school the next morning, Emmy caught the doll on her desk out of the corner of her eye. She remembered the haircut she had given it, but she had already forgotten just how far she had gone. Had she really chopped all the doll's hair off, and would that mean what she thought it would mean for Lizzy?

Oh, wow, she thought as she looked more closely at the uneven threads of yarn sticking out of the doll's scalp.

At lunchtime, as Emmy had predicted, Lizzy sat at her new spot alone in the cafeteria, her head covered in a big winter hat. Even from far away, Emmy could see that her food was spread on the table in front of her but she wasn't eating. She was just staring into space. She could also tell from far away that there was no hair poking out from under her hat. Emmy wanted to eavesdrop on Sophie and Cadence, who were deep in conversation at their usual table, so she pretended that she needed ketchup and got up to walk slowly past their table.

"I have no idea," Sophie was saying. "How can I even guess at the reasons she does what she does? She must have whacked out again, like she did at her sleepover."

"Well, we should go over there and see," Cadence replied. Emmy got her ketchup and went back to her table. She nibbled her grilled cheese and fries as she watched Sophie and Cadence approach Lizzy's table. Lizzy looked like she wanted to hide but was cornered, literally, in the cafeteria. Sophie and Cadence stood close to Lizzy. At first it looked like they were interrogating her and Lizzy wasn't answering. Then it looked like they were trying to grab the hat off of Lizzy's head, while Lizzy had her hands on it as if she was holding on for dear life. It was like watching television with the sound muted. Emmy wished she were sitting closer. Still, she had a pretty good view, just like she had a view into Lizzy's room from her own bedroom at home.

So when Cadence forcefully tugged the hat off Lizzy's

head, Emmy could clearly see what was underneath.

A whacked-out mess.

Lizzy's hair was all short, but some pieces were longer than others, giving the impression that her hair was sprouting in unimaginable ways.

Emmy watched Sophie and Cadence put their hands to their mouths in disbelief. She also saw half the lunchroom do the same as they slowly noticed the scene in the corner. Lizzy looked the way Emmy felt in that dream she sometimes had where she wasn't wearing any clothes in public. Exposed. Mortified. Lizzy saw Emmy staring and, for a moment, the two held each other's gaze. *You're finally getting what you deserve,* Emmy thought. *You deserve to be friendless.*

Then Emmy looked away.

For the rest of the day Emmy noticed that no one talked to Lizzy. They just pointed and laughed. She kept the hat on, but it was too late. Everyone had seen what was underneath. A whole lot of nothing with a little bit of crazy.

At the dinner table that night, Emmy was in an especially good mood. She stabbed happily at her salad with her fork as she and her parents listened to Sam describe the high and low of his day. His high was getting to be the line leader at recess, and his low was that his team lost a dodgeball game. Pretty different from Emmy's day. *Sam's life is so simple,* Emmy thought, putting aside her good mood for a second and hating him a little. She remembered when her life was that simple.

"How about you, Emmy?" her dad asked her when Sam had finished. Emmy stayed silent. She wasn't exactly eager to report to her family that the high point of her day was the unveiling of Lizzy's hair and her subsequent humiliation in front of the entire school. But it was true.

And now Emmy's mom was looking at her in a way that let Emmy know that she knew about Lizzy's hair. She must have talked to Lizzy's mom. Emmy felt a small stab of guilt. But of course, there was no way she could ever be blamed for the haircut, if you could even call it a haircut. Emmy remained silent.

"Well, there's an elephant in the room, it seems," her mom said.

"What are you talking about?" Sam said. "What elephant?"

"That means there's something that no one wants

to talk about, but it's obviously there," Emmy's dad explained patiently to Sam. "Right, Emmy?"

"I guess," Emmy said, now pushing her salad around her plate with her fork. She felt her parents' eyes on her as she looked down at her plate.

"Well, I talked to Marilyn on the phone today," Emmy's mom said. "What on earth do you think made Lizzy want to do that to her hair?"

Emmy started to respond when she suddenly began laughing uncontrollably. Her parents frowned. But she couldn't stop. There was an edge of hysteria to her laughter, and her eyes were starting to tear.

Her mom sighed. "I understand you feel hurt by the way Lizzy has been treating you lately, honey," she said. "But Marilyn said Lizzy's day was just horrible. She said everyone at school made fun of her and the teasing just wouldn't stop. She's been in her room crying all afternoon. I just can't imagine what she was thinking, cutting off all her pretty hair."

Her dad cleared his throat. "I'm very sorry to hear about Lizzy," he pointed out. "But, Emmy, I know you've been having a hard time too. Lizzy hasn't exactly been a good friend to you lately." Finally, a little understanding!

"Perhaps, Emmy, you are feeling a bit of schadenfreude," her mom added.

"Shaden-what?" Sam asked. His face wrinkled into a mask of confusion.

"Schadenfreude," Emmy's mom said. "*Sha-din-froy-duh*. It's a German word. It means taking pleasure in the misfortunes of others. Suppose one day in school someone trips you just to be mean. Then later that day he gets hurt on the playground. You might feel just a little bit glad that something bad happened to him, right?"

"I get it," Sam said. "So Emmy has schadenfreude?"

"I'm afraid so," her dad said. "It's not a feeling most of us would admit to, but it exists."

But even through the seriousness of the conversation, and the genuine understanding of her parents, Emmy couldn't stop laughing. Finally, her parents started to seem a little annoyed.

"Why don't you excuse yourself, Emmy?" her mom suggested.

Emmy could barely get the words out. "May I be excused?"

"You certainly may," her mom said.

Emmy brought her plate to the sink and walked upstairs to her room. She lay down on her bed and stared at the ceiling. *It's not schadenfreude,* she thought. *I'm just plain happy that I have the power to do this to Lizzy. And I don't need a big German word to describe it.* It was that simple.

Before breakfast, Emmy marched straight into her parents' bathroom, took her mom's makeup bag, brought it into her room, and locked the door. *Who knows why I'm locking the door,* she thought. *It's not like anyone knows anything about the doll.*

Emmy sat at her desk and stared at the doll. *What a doll.* Emmy had never felt this powerful. She imagined this is what witches must feel like. Schadenfreude or not, it felt amazing.

Lizzy's still pretty, even with her crazy hair, but I can fix that too, she thought.

Slowly, deliberately, Emmy put a smear of bright red lipstick on the doll's mouth. The doll was so small that the lipstick smudge was huge in comparison. Then she grabbed black eyeliner and outlined the doll's eyes. She followed up with blue eye shadow and blush, all applied clumsily because of how tiny the doll's face was. She examined her work. The only way to describe the way the doll looked now was clownish.

Emmy walked to school that morning with an extra spring in her step, knowing for sure what she'd see when she got there. And she was right.

Lizzy sat alone on the steps near the entrance to the school building. She looked like she'd been crying. But that wasn't the first thing that a person would notice about her. Her makeup looked as if a little kid had applied it. It looked utterly ridiculous. Combined with her winter hat, she looked bizarre. She stared at the ground as other kids stared at her. Some kids pointed, others whispered, others laughed.

One boy called out, "Hey, it's a crazy clown!"

Emmy walked right by Lizzy, trying not to stare, but unable not to. Lizzy looked up and their eyes met.

"Hi," Lizzy said softly.

Emmy's heart skipped a beat. Lizzy looked so sad and horrible.

"Hi," she muttered as she walked quickly past. Her chest tightened and she felt anxious. She had to get to her locker, and she felt like she had to get away from Lizzy.

As she spun the dial to unlock her locker, Emmy felt two distinctly different feelings wash over her.

The first was shame. *It was a terrible thing I did,* she thought. *Make that things I did. Did I really have to be so evil this morning? The sleepover and the hair were bad enough.*

The second was relief. *Lizzy's not popular anymore. Lizzy and I can be best friends again.* As the morning went on and she sat in her classes, Emmy imagined her reunion with Lizzy. She'd go to her table at lunch and sit with her—no one else would be sitting with her, she was sure of that.

At lunch, Emmy took a deep breath, carried her tray over to Lizzy's table, and sat across from her.

"Hey," she said, not looking at Lizzy.

"Hey," Lizzy said softly. She kept her eyes on the table. Her voice seemed hoarse. Maybe from crying.

"How are you?" Emmy asked. She didn't know what else to say.

"Are you serious?" Lizzy asked. But she didn't sound angry. She looked up and they finally made eye contact. "I'm kind of a mess, if you haven't noticed."

"I guess I did. A little," Emmy said. They sat in silence for a minute.

"I'm sorry everything is so awful right now," Emmy said. She really didn't know what else to say. But she did mean it—pretty much, anyway. Lizzy looked up.

"I'm really sorry about everything," Lizzy said softly, not looking at Emmy.

Emmy swallowed hard and stayed silent. She wanted to make up, but part of her had to admit it felt good having the upper hand like this. She was basically rescuing Lizzy from a friendless existence, after all.

"What do you mean, 'everything'?" she pressed.

"I mean, I'm sorry for being such a bad friend," Lizzy said. "I'm sorry I've been kind of ditching you this year."

"What else are you sorry for?" Emmy had to hear her say it.

"I'm sorry for cutting your hair short. Now I know how you felt. It wasn't right of me to do something you didn't want. But at least yours is longer than mine," she added.

"Thanks," Emmy said. "I'm sorry you're having such a hard time."

Lizzy smiled sheepishly.

Emmy realized there was one thing she really wanted to ask Lizzy. It was something she truly did not know the answer to. "Can I ask you a question?" she said.

"Sure," Lizzy said. "Ask me anything. I couldn't be more embarrassed than I already am."

"What were you thinking, cutting your hair in that way and putting on all this makeup?" Emmy asked. "Like, how did this happen?"

Lizzy sighed. "I don't know," she muttered. "Both times, I just got into a really weird mood. Like, I wasn't in control of myself. Both the haircut and the makeup seemed like perfectly good ideas at the time. But both times, when I was finished, I wondered what had come over me. And now I'm afraid I'm going crazy," Lizzy whispered, her eyes filling with tears.

"You're not going crazy," Emmy assured her. "You just got into a weird mood. Everyone gets into weird moods sometimes."

"I wish I could just wash this makeup off," Lizzy moaned. "But I've scrubbed and scrubbed and hardly any has come off."

Emmy made a mental note to wash the doll's face the first chance she got. It was time to end this, and she had another great idea for how to do that. "I know what you need to make you feel better," she said to Lizzy.

"A sleepover at my house this weekend. What do you think?"

Lizzy looked grateful. "I'd like that," she said, and wiped away her tears with a napkin. She smiled.

And just like that, they were back in the friendship nest. Just the two of them. Just two best friends planning a sleepover.

CHAPTER 10

After school Emmy raced straight to Zim Zam. She had to get rid of that doll right away. She didn't want to do any more damage. She had already done more than enough. And what would be the point, anyway? After all, she had her best friend back.

Emmy knew just what she was going to say when she returned the doll. She wouldn't ask for a refund, especially given the condition of the doll, with its butchered hair and the mess of makeup all over its face. And the money didn't matter. What mattered was getting that doll out of her house and out of her life. The doll clearly had supernatural powers and had to go directly back to where it came from. It also had to be reset. What happened to the doll could no longer also happen to Lizzy. Emmy didn't care what happened after that.

She would just tell the woman with the long white hair that she needed to return the doll to the place it had come from, and thank you very much, but she wouldn't be needing it anymore. She had a feeling the woman would understand exactly what she meant. She rehearsed what she was going to say as she entered Zim Zam to the familiar jingle of the bells on the door.

As usual, Zoom was there, as was Christine, who was busy ringing up some customers. Emmy knelt down to pet Zoom for a minute, but Zoom ran away hissing, so Emmy got up and headed over to the puppet display, looking for the door to the back room.

There it was, behind the puppets. But as she went to turn the knob, she saw a giant metal bolt on the door.

Emmy stood still for a moment, puzzled. Why was the room bolted closed? She approached Christine at the register. Christine was saying good-bye to the customers and thanking them, and Emmy patiently waited until Christine turned her attention to her.

"Hi, Emmy, what's the matter?" Christine asked her.

Was it that obvious how weirded out Emmy was? She supposed so.

"Um, I was just trying to get into that special back room," Emmy said. She suddenly felt very self-conscious.

"What do you mean?" Christine asked.

"The little back room I went into last time I was here," Emmy explained, trying to sound normal. "It's bolted shut today. But it had been open. I went in there."

Christine raised her eyebrows. "There's no back room here, sweetie," she said. "There's just this little closet behind the cash register. That's where I store all my things, like keys and office supplies." Christine stepped aside and opened a small closet filled with stuff. It was nothing like the little back room with the woman and the incense and the dolls. Emmy stared at the closet, then stared back at Christine, not having any idea what to say next.

"I was there last week," she finally said. "A woman with long white hair sold me a doll and gave me a candle. A lavender candle," she added, as if that would be of some help in solving this mystery.

"Maybe it was a dream," Christine said, trying to be helpful. "It sounds kind of like a dream."

Emmy's heart skipped a beat. It was as if Christine was telling her that maybe black was white and up was down. Emmy knew it hadn't been a dream. She had the doll to prove it.

What else could Emmy do? She swung her backpack around, unzipped the front pocket, and pulled out the little doll. She put it on the counter in front of Christine as hard evidence.

"This is what I bought," Emmy said, gesturing to the doll.

"What's this?" Christine said, picking it up. "We don't sell anything like this."

"It's what I bought," Emmy said again. "It cost four dollars and thirty-two cents. I remember because it's exactly how much money I had in my wallet that day. And the room was in the back, near the puppets."

"Oh, why didn't you say so!" Christine exclaimed, her face lighting up with sudden understanding.

Thank goodness I'm not going crazy, Emmy thought. *Christine does know what I'm talking about. She'll make everything make sense.*

"I know what you mean now," Christine continued. "Yes, there *is* a door back there. Of course. It's been there for as long as I've owned the store. I think it used to connect Zim Zam to the store next door. But that store's been closed forever, and anyway, the landlord told me to never open that door, so I don't. Even if I wanted to, I don't have the key."

Emmy's heart sank. Christine didn't know what Emmy was talking about after all. "No, I-I was in there," she stammered. "It's a whole separate store, with a woman selling things."

Christine was nodding kindly, as if Emmy were a small child telling a tall tale. "It really sounds like a dream, sweetie," she said again. "And the doll came from somewhere else, somewhere you don't remember. You have lots of toys and dolls and stuffed animals at home, right? And you don't remember exactly where each one came from, right?"

Emmy felt her face get hot. "Yeah," she said, pretending to go along with Christine's dream theory, because what else could she say or do now? She stuffed the doll back in the front pocket of her backpack and left Zim Zam as fast as she could.

Once outside, she gasped for breath. She walked around the building, and then the block, to see if there was another way to get into the little shop. Nothing.

Emmy felt crazy. She had to go back into Zim Zam and look again. Christine was busy with another customer, and once more Zoom arched his back and hissed at Emmy as she entered.

Like she had the first time, Emmy slid behind the rack of puppets and got close to the door. Close enough to see something that chilled her to the bone.

It was something etched into the wood above the bolt. Words.

And the words were, "I'm watching you, Emmy."

Emmy stood stiffly and stared at the words. A million thoughts rushed through her head at once. *Who had written these words? The old woman?* She'd seemed nice, but then Emmy remembered how the woman had gotten Emmy to admit that she *hated* Lizzy, which she never would have done if the woman hadn't pushed her in that direction. Emmy's mind began to race.

What did the woman know about the doll? What was her purpose in selling me the doll? Was it to test if I was a good person or not?

And what about that lavender candle? Why was it so important that I light the candle? Did the candle activate a spell that, besides controlling Lizzy's behavior, also controlled mine? Have I been controlled by the doll too? Was that why I suddenly turned into such a mean, spiteful person who hurt my best friend and spied on her, and took such pleasure in seeing her suffer?

She had to get out of there. Christine was still busy with a customer and had probably never even seen her walk in again in the first place. Emmy walked slowly home, reminding herself to breathe.

She had so many questions, but she knew one thing: It wasn't going to be so easy to get rid of this doll. And now she knew for sure that no good could come from keeping it.

CHAPTER 11

Emmy walked home feeling superaware of the doll's presence in her backpack. The doll may as well have been on fire in there; that's how aware Emmy was of it. What was she going to do with it now?

Well, tomorrow was garbage day. Emmy knew this because it was her job to take out the garbage to the sidewalk every week. She also knew that the biggest, deepest garbage can in the house was in the kitchen. It was also the grossest—full of eggshells, coffee grounds, and apple cores. If she stuffed the doll deep in there, no one would find it and it would be out of the house before she went to bed that night. And it would be totally gone early tomorrow morning when the trash was picked up.

Emmy felt a little bit better as she imagined herself

asleep that night, slightly awakened by the noisy rumble of the garbage truck. She thought about how she would feel hearing it drive away, knowing what it was carrying inside. She usually found that sound annoying because it woke her up, but this time it would be a welcome annoyance. She imagined the doll ending up at a big dump where no one would ever possess it again.

Okay, step one, she thought. Following through with her plan, Emmy went into the kitchen and looked around. Was anyone around? Sam was upstairs, her dad was in his office, and her mom was still at work. Okay. The coast was clear. Emmy fished the doll out of her backpack. Then she held it in front of her. "You are not Lizzy," she said to the doll, hoping that would break the curse. Finally, she shoved the doll down as far as she could into the garbage can. Her stomach turned as she reached through all the gross garbage. She couldn't wait to wash her hands, which she did immediately.

Suddenly Sam was behind her. Emmy jumped. "What were you doing digging in the garbage?" he asked. She hadn't heard him come in.

"Why are you so nosy?" she snapped at him. She hadn't meant to sound so harsh, but the thought of anyone knowing anything about that doll sort of sent her over the edge.

"I'm not," Sam said defensively. "I'm just asking."

"I thought I dropped my bracelet in there by accident, so I was digging around for it," Emmy lied quickly.

"Oh," Sam said. "Did you find it?"

"Um, no," Emmy said.

"Well, the garbage doesn't gross me out," Sam said. "Do you want me to keep digging in there for it?"

Emmy felt bad for speaking to him so sharply. She tried to soften her voice.

"It's okay, I think I lost it somewhere else," she said. "But thanks."

There were still a couple more days of school before the weekend, and Emmy and Lizzy ate lunch together both days. Lizzy was looking a little better. She'd gotten a stylish black hat to replace her big clumsy winter hat. And the other kids seemed to have lost interest in making fun of her hair, or lack thereof. Lizzy looked like she'd finally gotten some sleep, and though she seemed a little sad about not sitting with Sophie and Cadence—Emmy caught her glancing over at their table a few times—she was acting a lot more like her old self. Both days, when it came time to exit the lunchroom, the two girls walked the long way around the room so they wouldn't have to walk directly by Sophie and Cadence. Emmy still felt guilty for what she'd done, but reminded herself that Sophie and Cadence hadn't been good friends to Lizzy anyway.

Friday night finally rolled around and Lizzy came over before dinner. As Emmy opened the front door, a warm feeling came over her. She had missed Lizzy so much. She was so happy to be having this sleepover— and so glad she hadn't done any permanent damage with the doll. Lizzy was still on crutches, of course, but her leg was going to heal completely, and her hair would grow back, Emmy told herself. Just as Emmy's would.

And normal is exactly how things felt as Emmy and Lizzy sat at the dinner table with Emmy's family, eating lasagna and sharing highs and lows of their days as usual.

"How about you, Lizzy?" Emmy's mom asked. "What were the high and low of your day?"

"Well, I know the low," Lizzy said quickly. "The low is every morning when I wake up and look in the bathroom mirror at my crazy hair. My hairdresser tried to fix it, but it's just not right yet. I guess it'll just have to grow out."

Emmy's mom nodded sympathetically. "That must be hard," she said. "And it will grow back, honey. Too bad we can't say the same for you, dear," she said with a grin to Emmy's dad.

"Very funny," Emmy's dad said sarcastically. "So what are you two up to tonight? I seem to remember that not much slumber goes on at your slumber parties." It was true. They usually would stay up quite late and Emmy's parents would have to shush them a few times.

"Crispy rice pizza, of course," Emmy said, and she and Lizzy both giggled. Just hearing those words together was hilarious. Emmy had seen the recipe on the side of the cereal box and brought it to school that day to show Lizzy. You made a batch of regular crispy rice cereal treats, then pressed them onto a pizza pan. You melted more marshmallows, stirred in red food coloring, and spread that on top for sauce. Then you added coconut to look like cheese, and chocolate chips for the pizza topping. You sliced it up just like a pizza. She couldn't wait to make it. She was in such a good mood, she figured she'd even share the finished product with Sam. Then again, she didn't want her little brother to interfere with her perfectly good evening.

"Another one of your crazy concoctions?" Emmy's mom said. "Well, just be sure to clean up after yourselves."

"We will," Emmy reassured her mom. "Anyway, may we be excused?" She thought they'd go up to her room and brainstorm costumes. The costume party was only a week away, and they'd better get going with their ideas if they wanted their costumes to be any good.

"Sure," Emmy's mom said, and Lizzy and Emmy went up to Emmy's room and closed the door. No sooner had they done so then Sam barged right in, wanting to be a part of things.

"Ever heard of knocking?" Emmy said to Sam.

"Sorry," Sam said. "I wondered if you guys wanted to play zoo."

"Not tonight," Emmy said. "It's girls' night. And please don't barge in here again."

Sam turned and left without a word.

"I hate it when he does that," Emmy said to Lizzy. "I'm making a sign." She went to her desk, took a piece of paper and a thick purple magic marker, and wrote

NO LITTLE BROTHERS ALLOWED! in big block letters. Then she tore two pieces of tape off the roll, put the sign on her door, and closed it again.

"There," she said. "We should be safe now."

Lizzy laughed. "I don't mind," she said. "But then again I don't know how annoying it can be to have a brother or sister."

"It can be very annoying, I promise you," Emmy said. "Now, let's make a list of costume possibilities. I have one. Bacon and eggs."

Lizzy laughed again. "I love it," she said as Emmy wrote it down. "Okay, here's another one. Paint can and paintbrush." Emmy wrote that down, too.

Lizzy's face lit up. "Raggedy Ann and Raggedy Andy!" she said, referring to two dolls they used to play with when they were little. But the very thought of dolls freaked Emmy out and she tried to think of another idea quickly, even as she wrote that one down.

"I think dolls would be kind of creepy, actually," Emmy said.

"Really? Why?" Lizzy asked.

"Oh, I don't know," Emmy said. "The way clowns are creepy. I just think dolls are creepy."

"Raggedy Ann and Andy would be easy costumes to make," Lizzy said. She was obviously in love with the idea. "And we don't have much time before the party."

"Hey, how about we start on the pizza?" Emmy asked suddenly, putting down her pencil and notebook. Maybe Lizzy would forget all about the doll costume idea.

The girls went downstairs and started getting set up for cooking. Emmy got the marshmallows, butter, and box of cereal out of the pantry and put a big pot on the stove. She turned the heat on low and added the marshmallows and butter.

"Can you stir this while I get out the other stuff?" she asked Lizzy. Lizzy smiled, took the wooden spoon, and began stirring. Emmy got out food coloring, coconut, and chocolate chips and set them on the kitchen counter for the next step. As she did so, though, she heard a familiar whine.

"I want to help!" Sam was suddenly standing in the kitchen. His expression was part hurt, part angry.

"I told you it was girls' night," Emmy told him.

"It's okay," Lizzy said. "He can help."

"No, he can't," Emmy said. After everything she and

Lizzy had been through, she just wanted some alone time with her best friend. Was that too much to ask? "He'll mess everything up." Sam turned and left without a fight.

By then the marshmallow and butter had melted together. Emmy poured in the dry cereal as Lizzy stirred hard, and then they poured the hot mixture onto a pizza pan. They used their hands to press the mixture down until it looked like a pizza crust. Emmy forgot all about her annoying little brother.

"Okay, now for the best part," Emmy said, "The sauce. We melt more marshmallows and butter together with red food coloring. Want to stir again?"

"Yup," Lizzy said. It really was just like old times.

The mixture looked totally gross, like blood. Lizzy stirred it quickly so it wouldn't burn.

"Ow!" she said suddenly.

"What?" Emmy said, looking at her. Lizzy was grimacing and holding her neck.

"What's the matter?" Emmy asked again.

"I suddenly got a really bad cramp in my neck," Lizzy said. Emmy could tell she was in real pain.

"Weird," Emmy said sympathetically.

"I know," Lizzy said. "I've never had a cramp like this before."

Suddenly they heard a voice behind them. Both girls practically jumped out of their skin. But it was just Sam again. So annoying!

"What's the matter?" he asked.

Emmy turned around to see what he wanted. He was holding something in his hands. Something that looked a little too familiar to Emmy. The doll! And he was gripping it in a way that looked like he was trying to rip its head off. Which, Emmy remembered, he was once very fond of doing to her Barbie dolls.

Everything began to move in slow motion for Emmy. She could feel her heart beat in her ears. She rushed over to Sam and pulled him out of the room so Lizzy wouldn't see what was in his hands or hear the horror in her voice. "Where did you get that?" she hissed, grabbing the doll from Sam's grip. She was so terrified that she almost felt as if she were outside her own body, watching this all happen. She examined the doll carefully. A few stitches were loose around the doll's neck, but thank goodness nothing worse.

"In the garbage," Sam replied. "It's perfectly good,"

he added. "Why did you throw it away?"

"It's none of your business," she said, stuffing the doll quickly into her pocket before she went back to the kitchen. "Are you okay?" she asked Lizzy.

"Yeah, the cramp went away," Lizzy said, no longer clutching her own neck.

"That's good," Emmy said, both relieved and totally freaked out.

"What was that about?" Lizzy asked, as she absent-mindedly continued to stir the sauce mixture.

"Nothing," Emmy said, trying not to sound as scared as she was. "Just be glad you don't have a little brother."

Emmy heard footsteps behind them and she spun around and glared at Sam, who had dared to return to the kitchen. "Get out of here," Emmy scolded. What a horrifyingly close call. She couldn't even imagine the scene if Sam had actually been successful in ripping the head off, though of course that wouldn't have been as easy to do as it was on a Barbie doll. "And stay away from my stuff," she added.

"I wasn't even in your stuff! I found it in the garbage!" Sam retorted.

"Okay. Please just leave us alone," Emmy said,

calming down a bit. She had to hold it together in front of Lizzy. Lizzy would wonder why Emmy was coming undone the way she was. Sam left the room.

The doll is safe in my pocket, Emmy told herself. *As long as I keep it in my pocket nothing else bad can happen.* She was beginning to breathe normally.

"So what now?" Lizzy asked Emmy.

"What do you mean?" Emmy replied. What *was* she going to do? Clearly she hadn't broken the spell on the doll. How would she ever get rid of that doll once and for all?

"What's the next step?" Lizzy asked. It was then that Emmy realized Lizzy was talking about the recipe and wasn't going to press her any more about what had just happened.

"Oh." She laughed in a way that she hoped sounded completely casual. "We spread the red stuff on the pizza to look like sauce. Wanna do it?"

"Sure." Lizzy smiled. Emmy watched her friend use a rubber spatula to scrape the red mixture out of the pot and onto the pizza, where she spread it around evenly to look like a pizza with sauce on it. She couldn't take her eyes off the red gooey stuff as she thought about what might have happened if Sam had actually beheaded the doll. Her stomach turned. It was all Emmy could do to keep herself from getting sick.

Once Lizzy was finished spreading the sauce, Emmy sprinkled shredded coconut on the pizza to look like shredded cheese. She tried hard to act like everything was normal, and tried to put out of her mind the thought of what could have happened.

"Let's do the chocolate chips together," Lizzy suggested. They were really in a groove, Emmy thought. They were working together just like old times. It was going to be okay. Emmy just had to calm down and not think about what could have happened. They pressed the chocolate chips into the pizza and admired their creation.

"I know!" Lizzy said suddenly. "Do you have any gummy fish? We can use them for anchovies."

Emmy grinned. What a brilliant idea. She was starting to breathe a little more normally now. "I'll go check," she said. Emmy's mom usually didn't keep much candy in the house, but she did have a sweet tooth for the little red gummy fish. Emmy went into the pantry where Lizzy couldn't see her.

Once in the pantry Emmy pulled the doll out of her pocket and stared at it. It was eerie how similar its hair looked to Lizzy's actual hair. The makeup was totally smudged and dirty, but still evident. Luckily Lizzy had been able to wipe the makeup off her own face, but what on earth would she have thought if she had seen the doll? She would have had a lot of questions about why Emmy was carrying around a freaky doll, that was for certain. Emmy felt flooded with relief that Lizzy was clueless about what had just happened.

Emmy shoved the doll back into her pocket. It was the only safe place for now.

"Emmy?" Lizzy called from the kitchen. "What are you doing in there?"

Emmy took a deep breath and grabbed a small plastic bag full of the gummy fish. She stepped out of the closet, holding them up triumphantly.

"Just getting the anchovies!" She giggled. "Come on, let's add them to the pizza." They went to work arranging them.

The finished product looked colorful, sugary, and awesome. Emmy took a pizza cutter out of the utensil drawer and started slicing it just like a real pizza. It was still a little warm. She handed the first slice to Lizzy, who took a big bite.

"Mmm," Lizzy said appreciatively. "You have to try it."

Emmy picked up her slice and took a bite. As the sticky sweetness filled her mouth, she thought of how sour this night could have become. *But it didn't,* she reminded herself, forcing a smile at Lizzy. *I got to the doll in time. It didn't.*

CHAPTER 12

Later that night Emmy lay in her bed in the dark as Lizzy lay on the floor in her sleeping bag. With the exception of the doll, all seemed right with the world to Emmy. Here was her best friend, lying in her bedroom like she had a million times before.

"I've been thinking," Lizzy began.

Oh no, Emmy thought. Then she reassured herself. *Lizzy knows nothing about the doll.* She had put the doll in her night-table drawer while Lizzy was in the bathroom getting ready for bed.

"I really think we should be Raggedy Ann and Andy for the costume party," Lizzy continued. "The costumes would be really easy to make, and I could wear a wig made of red yarn."

Emmy paused. Just the idea of yarn hair on Lizzy made her skin crawl. "I just think it's kind of babyish," Emmy said. She knew that would make the idea a lot less attractive to Lizzy.

"I guess you're right," Lizzy said. "Okay, but we really have to think of something great."

"We will," Emmy assured her friend. "For sure."

Emmy listened as Lizzy began to fall asleep. She lay there thinking of how much she'd hurt Lizzy. Yes, Lizzy had hurt her too, but now Emmy was overcome with guilt at the havoc she'd wreaked in Lizzy's life. A broken leg! Crazy hair! And more, of course. She had to get rid of that doll as soon as Lizzy left in the morning. And she had to make sure that the spell was no longer on it.

When she was sure that Lizzy was deep asleep, Emmy slipped out of bed, grabbed the doll from her night-table drawer, and quietly padded over to her desk. She sat down in the chair, in front of the lavender candle. She knew her mother had asked her not to burn the candle without her supervision, but Emmy didn't have a choice.

Emmy lit the candle. She watched as its flame danced to life and then she turned her attention to the doll.

"I don't hate you, Lizzy," she whispered over and over

again, so silently that Emmy could barely hear herself. And then, "You are no longer Lizzy. I release you."

The flame started flickering. Emmy could only hope that she had broken the curse she had unintentionally put on this now-tattered doll and on her best friend. And this time she knew she had to test it out before she tried to get rid of the doll.

Emmy turned her chair so she was staring at Lizzy as she slept peacefully, wrapped up in her cozy sleeping bag. Emmy started waving the doll's arms around wildly. Lizzy didn't move.

Emmy made the little doll dance, but again Lizzy didn't move.

Emmy let out a sigh of relief that was so forceful, it blew out the flame on the candle. Her hunch had been right. The candle and the doll were somehow connected. And she had broken the spell.

Now all she had to do was wait until morning when Lizzy left to go home. It would be a long, sleepless night, but tomorrow she would get rid of the doll once and for all. It didn't have any powers anymore, but all the same, Emmy wanted it gone. For good.

As Emmy had feared, it was a rough stretch till morning. She'd fall into a light sleep for a little while but then wake right up. Each time she did, she wanted to check the night-table drawer to make sure the doll was still there, but she didn't want to wake up Lizzy. Finally, the sun came up and the room turned light. Emmy tried to talk herself through her anxiety. *Lizzy will leave right after breakfast and I'll walk down to the river. I'll throw the doll into the water and watch it sink. And it will be gone, gone forever. And Lizzy will never find out about what I've done to her, and we'll stay best friends forever. Her hair will grow back and her leg will heal and everything will be fine.*

Emmy lay there impatiently waiting for Lizzy to open her eyes. She could already hear her parents downstairs making coffee and preparing breakfast. She heard Sam go downstairs and wanted to go downstairs too—she'd been in this bed long enough—but didn't want to leave the doll in the room alone with sleeping Lizzy. She did little things to wake Lizzy up, like cough and rock her bed so it squeaked. Finally, Lizzy stirred.

"Mmmm," she said, her eyes still closed. Lizzy was such a heavy sleeper.

"Morning, Lizard," Emmy said, using her old nickname for Lizzy.

"I'm not a lizard," Lizzy said, her eyes still closed, but a smile on her face.

"Sorry, Lizard," Emmy replied. Finally, Lizzy opened her eyes.

"Did I sleep too late?" Lizzy said, rubbing her eyes.

"No, you're fine," Emmy said. "You have an hour before your mom wants you to be home. Let's go downstairs and get breakfast."

Emmy and Lizzy got up slowly and shuffled their way down to the kitchen in their pajamas.

"Hi, pizza makers," Emmy's dad said. Emmy and Lizzy both smiled sleepily, proud of their creation, half of which was currently on the kitchen table. Sam sat at the table too, eating a slice.

"Mom said this counts as breakfast," he told the girls, obviously very pleased with his mother's judgment.

"For sure it does," Emmy said, trying to act normal around him. She just wanted to put last night, and the past two weeks, behind her. She was still so freaked out about what could have happened while they were making the sauce.

Emmy and Lizzy both poured themselves big bowls of cereal and dug in.

"What do you plan to do today, Emmy?" her mom asked. "Lizzy, I know you have plans with your family. I told your mom I'd make sure to send you home in time."

"I'm not sure," Emmy answered. Though, of course, she was totally sure. She had to get to the river, which was more like a canal actually, and a good twenty blocks from her house. Still, she had to do it alone, so she couldn't very well ask her parents for a ride.

After breakfast when Lizzy had to go, she turned to Emmy and gave her a hug, and they stayed in the hug an extra long time.

"I'm glad we had a sleepover," Lizzy said, a little shyly.

"Me too," Emmy said. But there was so much that neither of them was saying.

I'm so glad we're friends again. I'm so sorry I hurt you. Let's never let that happen again.

As soon as Lizzy left, Emmy ran upstairs and pulled on sweatpants, a sweatshirt, and sneakers as fast as she could. She opened the night-table drawer, took out the doll, and put it into her sweatpants pocket. Then she walked downstairs, reminding herself to act normally.

"I'm going for a walk," she told her parents, who were still at the breakfast table reading the newspaper.

"To where?" her dad said. Taking a random walk wasn't something Emmy usually did.

"Um, I have to go to the park and look for certain wildflowers for art class," she lied. "We're doing some kind of big art project next week." She was pretty impressed with her own story. It was foolproof.

"That sounds fun," her mom said. "Want some company?"

"No!" Emmy said, a little too quickly and forcefully. "I mean, thanks, but I was looking forward to going by myself. Now that you let me walk places outside by myself during the day," she added.

"Okay then," her mom said. "Have a good time, honey. Come right back home when you're done."

"I will," Emmy promised. She pulled on a light coat and stepped outside. The walk seemed to take forever. She kept one hand on the doll in her pocket. This was going to be it, the final farewell, and she couldn't mess it up.

Finally, she reached the river. It was called the Gowanus Canal, and it had the distinction of being one of the most polluted body of water in the country.

Emmy hoped that the toxic chemicals in the water would destroy the doll before it even sank to the bottom.

Even the birds floating on the water seemed dirty. "Oscar the Grouch's Riviera," her parents liked to call it jokingly. It was lined with dumps and junkyards and old abandoned warehouses. Emmy walked onto the bridge that crossed it and looked down.

She took the doll out of her pocket and looked at it one last time. Then she took a deep breath and hurled it as hard as she could into the murky water below. It fell with a satisfying *plop*. She felt immediate relief as she watched it sink deeper and deeper until she couldn't see it anymore. The water was so dark that it quickly obscured the doll. She stayed for a minute, still a little afraid to turn her back on the thing, until she finally made herself turn around and start walking.

Emmy felt like a weight had been lifted off her chest. Her life was going to be normal again! Lizzy was her best friend and the doll with the crazy powers was gone, gone, gone. She felt so proud of herself, like she'd accomplished something remarkable. Lizzy was none the wiser, and she'd solved the problem all by herself. *All's well that ends well,* she thought.

She was actually going to have a regular day, her first in awhile. She reminded herself to look for flowers on the way home so her story would hold up. She felt like skipping straight home, but turned around for one last look to be sure the doll was really gone. Better to be safe than sorry, she told herself.

And what she saw made her heart stop.

It was the old woman from the shop, sitting on the dock below.

She was holding the dripping doll in one hand and a lit candle in the other. A net sat beside her. The candle flickered but stayed lit against the wind. The woman's long, straggly white hair blew in the wind, and she looked like she was talking to the doll. Emmy couldn't hear her, but she was close enough that she could see the woman moving her lips. And she could definitely see her mole.

What she was saying was "Emmy, Emmy, Emmy."

Her name. The spell that activated the curse. Emmy remembered saying Lizzy's name when she first got this evil little doll.

Emmy stood frozen in place, unable to take her eyes off the woman. What should she do? Approach the woman and explain that she needed to get rid of the doll? Run away as fast as she could? She had no idea, and remained as still as a statue as she stared down at the woman, who was now looking up and smiling strangely.

Her smile in the shop had been friendly, but now it seemed like a mean kind of smile. Emmy gave her a halfhearted wave.

"Oh, Emmy?" the woman called up.

Emmy's heart skipped a beat. What could this woman have to say to her now?

Nothing, it turned out. Instead, the woman snapped a strand of the doll's hair in two. She had to tug hard since the yarn was thick.

And as the woman did so, Emmy felt a small but sharp pain on her head, the way it feels when a single piece of hair is tugged.

Because that's exactly what was happening.

"Ow!" Emmy cried. Her hand went instinctively to her head. The woman laughed and went back to pulling on the doll's hair.

Emmy started to run toward the woman, but the woman was too quick. She got up and started running at a pace far too fast for an ordinary elderly woman. But

Emmy knew by now that she was anything but ordinary. She was evil and she was also too fast for Emmy. Emmy soon lost her in the crowd on the bustling avenue. As she walked home, Emmy could feel the same small, sharp pains on her head, over and over again.

And by the time she walked in her front door, her hair was already shorter on one side of her head, and she was holding a clump of broken ends of hair in her hands.

EPILOGUE

The next morning Emmy's face was swollen from crying as she and Sam sat at the breakfast table with their parents. Since last night, Emmy's hair had gotten shorter and shorter. Her scalp felt sore from the constant tugging at her hair. She had no idea how to make the spell go away.

"We'll call Dr. Lewis today," her mom reassured her. Dr. Lewis was her pediatrician. "I'm sure there's a perfectly good explanation for what's happening to your hair."

Emmy knew that there was. But how could she explain this to her parents? She imagined trying to tell the doctor what had happened: *Well, see, I bought this doll from an old woman in a store, and it's like a voodoo doll. And I* used it to do terrible things to my friend. And it's been controlling me and making me do terrible things. And now the woman who sold it to me has put me under the doll's spell, and that's why my hair keeps falling out, but not in clumps, just one strand at a time.

Her dad tried to change the subject. "What do you kids have going on today? It's beautiful outside. Maybe we should go for a walk in the park."

"I'm going to stay home and read," Sam said.

"I'm going to take a nap," Emmy said.

A nap would be the only escape from the horror of reality. Emmy's eyes filled with tears. Again.

"Let me call the doctor right now, honey," her mom said sympathetically, pushing her chair away from the table. "He'll be able to figure out what's going on with your hair."

"Definitely," her dad added reassuringly.

Emmy went upstairs to her room and looked out her window into Lizzy's room. Lizzy was still asleep in her bed.

She never knew anything, Emmy thought, jealous of the peacefulness with which Lizzy rested. *And I know everything. And now it's my turn.*

DO NOT FEAR—
WE HAVE ANOTHER CREEPY TALE FOR YOU!

TURN THE PAGE FOR A SNEAK PEEK AT

You're invited to a

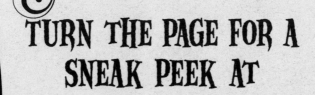

Read It and Weep!

The babysitter checked the clock again. Past eleven. They'd promised to be home by ten thirty. She shifted sleepily in the deep leather chair and glanced back at the TV. She had it turned down low, to an old black-and-white movie, which was quaintly spooky. Practically every scene included ominous music, sinister characters wearing hats and trench coats, and lots of fog and shadows. But she wasn't the sort of girl that got scared easily.

Outside, the wind howled, rattling the old doors and window frames. The draft caused the heavy floor-to-ceiling drapes to billow, as though someone were hiding behind them. The rain streamed down the windows in rivulets.

Lightning flashed. For a brief instant, through the gap in the drapery, the girl could see the dark landscape illuminated outside—black trees bending, empty swings bobbing crazily in the wind. There was a loud crack of thunder.

And then the power went out.

With a blip the TV powered off. The reading lamp next to her went black. The girl was plunged into darkness, not complete blackness, but pretty close. With an exasperated sigh she stood up from the chair and groped her way toward the kitchen, shuffling with baby steps so as not to trip over any toys. Now she wished she'd done a better job of picking up after the twin girls, who'd been playing with their wooden food and plastic oven earlier that evening.

The kitchen was full of gray shadows and devoid of noise, except for the howling wind and pattering rain outside. There was no hum of the refrigerator. No whooshing of the dishwasher, which she'd actually remembered to turn on. Opening the drawer near the stove, she felt around for a flashlight. She came up with the next best thing—a candle, with a little holder attached. Luckily the gas stove worked, so she didn't have to search for matches and could light the candle. The weak flame flickered, shedding a wan light around her. And then she saw them:

A pair of green, glowing eyes, staring at her from the shadowy corner of the kitchen.

She gasped. Took a step backward, almost dropping the candle.

Then she exhaled.

"Nero! You dumb cat. You scared the life out of me."

She heard the orange-and-white tabby cat jump down from the counter and pad over to her, twining itself around her feet, purring.

Inside the pocket of her sweatshirt she felt her phone vibrate. She drew it out and checked the message. Another text.

I see you. You're in the kitchen. You're wearing a pink zip-up sweatshirt.

Her mouth went dry and her palms felt sweaty as she read the mysterious message. This was the third text she'd gotten tonight from that number. She scrolled back to reread the first two messages.

I'm back.

The second one was even creepier:

You thought you'd gotten rid of me. Well, you didn't. Your luck has changed.

This third one was deeply unsettling. She couldn't pass it off as a wrong number. She *was* wearing a pink sweatshirt. She *was* standing in the kitchen. How could someone possibly know that? She peered out of the window over the kitchen sink, straining her eyes to see past the streams of water running down. But all she could see was the blackness outside. All she could hear was the howling wind and the pattering rain. The kitchen faced the back of the house, where there was a small yard and then a grove of trees. No one in her right mind would be standing out there on a night like this. She set the candle down and texted back.

Whoever this is, cut it out. You're starting to freak me out.

Almost immediately, there was another text.

They're not coming home. Not anytime soon.

Fear eddied up and down her spine. Who were "they"? The twins' parents? She decided not to ask. This entire thing was as ridiculous as it was scary. She tried to convince herself that someone was just playing a practical joke on her. Her brothers or maybe her best friend.

A full two minutes passed without another text. The babysitter busied herself around the kitchen, trying to tidy it up as best she could in the darkness. Where were the parents? Why hadn't they called her to say they'd be late?

And then she got another text.

I am in the basement.

Her breath caught in her throat. This really wasn't funny anymore. Suddenly she realized it wasn't someone playing a practical joke on her. No one she knew would do something like this. Play such a mean trick. She'd call her mom. And then maybe even 911. But when she looked at her phone, she saw the worst possible message of all:

No service.

Wait. What was that sound?

Clomp. Clomp. Clomp.

At first she thought the sound was only in her imagination. But as it got louder, there was no mistaking the sound of footsteps. Then they stopped. She whirled around toward the basement door, which was shrouded in shadow. The door rattled. But that was the wind, wasn't it? Making it rattle?

She heard footsteps again, and a tiny, terrified whimper escaped from the back of her throat. Heavy footfalls continued making their way up the basement steps. And then slowly, ever so slowly, the knob on the basement door started to turn. When it opened, she saw what she'd been dreading—a figure covered in shadow. And then it started moving toward her.

WANT MORE CREEPINESS?

Then you're in luck, because P. J. Night has some more scares for you and your friends!

Write Your Own Horror Haiku

In the story, Emmy and Lizzy each write a haiku in their English class. Haiku poems have three lines. The first line has five syllables, the second line has seven syllables, and the third line has five syllables. P. J. Night wants you to write some haiku on the spaces below, but there's a catch: They have to be about something spooky. P. J. has written one to share with you. Share *your* horror haiku with your friends!

> *It can be spooky,*
> *Living in a haunted house.*
> *What's that over there?*

YOU'RE INVITED TO . . .
CREATE YOUR OWN SCARY STORY!

Do you want to turn your sleepover into a creepover? Telling a spooky story is a great way to set the mood. P. J. Night has written a few sentences to get you started. Fill in the rest of the story and have fun scaring your friends.

You can also collaborate with your friends on this story by taking turns. Have everyone at your sleepover sit in a circle. Pick one person to start. She will add a sentence or two to the story, cover what she wrote with a piece of paper leaving only the last word or phrase visible, and then pass the story to the next girl. Once everyone has taken a turn, read the scary story you created together aloud!

My best friend and I do everything together. One night, we even slept over at a real haunted house! It all started when my older sister told us about the strange things that had started happening at her friend's house. Objects were moving on their own, it would suddenly get chilly for no reason, and my sister's friend would hear whispering when she entered a room. So one night, my sister dared us to come along for a sleepover at her friend's house. We didn't get one wink of sleep all night. Instead we met the ghosts that were living there. They wanted to tell us their story. And it went like this . . .

_____

_____

_____

_____

_____

_____

_____

_____

THE END

A lifelong night owl, **P. J. NIGHT** often works furiously into the wee hours of the morning, writing down spooky tales and dreaming up new stories of the supernatural and otherworldly. Although P. J.'s whereabouts are unknown at this time, we suspect the author lives in a drafty, old mansion where the floorboards creak when no one is there and the flickering candlelight creates shadows that creep along the walls. We truly wish we could tell you more, but we've been sworn to keep P. J.'s identity a secret . . . and it's a secret we will take to our graves!

What's better than reading a really spooky story?

Writing your own!

You just read a great book. It gave you ideas, didn't it? Ideas for your next story: characters…plot…setting… You can't wait to grab a notebook and a pen and start writing it all down.

It happens a lot. *Ideas just pop into your head.* In between classes entire story lines take shape in your imagination. And when you start writing, the words flow, and you end up with notebooks crammed with your creativity.

It's okay, you aren't alone. Come to **KidPub**, the web's largest gathering of kids just like you. Share your stories with thousands of people from all over the world. Meet new friends and see what they're writing. Test your skills in one of our writing contests. See what other kids think about your stories.

And above all, *come to write!*

www.KidPub.com

DEAR KNOW-IT-ALL!

MARTONE SAYS
SCHOOL YEAR OFF
TO GOOD START

ARE YOU READY TO TURN UP YOUR
CREEP-O-METER?

Visit **CreepoverBooks.com**
for more super spooky activities,
excerpts, the series trailer, and
everything you need for throwing
the perfect creepover!

Simon
Spotlight